MOBILE LIBRARY

The Mobile Library visits three sites each day. A list
of them is available on request. Books must be returned
to the site from which they are borrowed. 50

DATE OF RETURN	DATE OF RETURN	DATE OF RETURN
25 NOV	29 JUL 1977	FICTION RESERVE
8 JAN 197	26 SEP 1977	
5 FEB 1976	11/77	71
2/76 INGOL	IBL FROM NE(FR? TO BG DB 1-4-94	
21 APR 1976	29 MAR 1994	
2 JUN 1976		
23 JUN 1976 9/76		
18 OCT 1976		
8 NOV 1976		
9 DEC 1976 3/77		
15 APR 1977		

J.C.&S./10,000/5/71

JACK OF EAGLES

by the same author

AFTER SUCH KNOWLEDGE
i   Doctor Mirabilis
ii (a) Black Easter
    (b) The Day After Judgement
iii A Case of Conscience

CITIES IN FLIGHT
i   They Shall Have Stars
ii A Life for the Stars
iii Earthman, Come Home
iv A Clash of Cymbals

BEST SCIENCE FICTION OF JAMES BLISH
THE SEEDLING STARS
A TORRENT OF FACES (with Norman L. Knight)

THE STAR DWELLERS
WELCOME TO MARS !
ANYWHEN
AND ALL THE STARS A STAGE

JACK
OF EAGLES

JAMES BLISH

FABER AND FABER
3 Queen Square London

First published in England in 1973
by Faber and Faber Limited
3 Queen Square London W.C.1
Printed in Great Britain by
John Dickens & Co Ltd Northampton
All rights reserved

ISBN 0 571 10276 X

". . . the time of experience, apprehended with true freshness, . . . consists of a blurred sequence of memories, culminating in the budding and unfolding present. . . . An integral component of this budding and unfolding present is an attitude of expectancy toward the future, no matter what it brings. . . . If someone could invent a figure for speaking of the flight of time, in which the idea is prominent that in our thought we recognize that the germinating present contains the seeds of a complete break with the past, he might alter the future course of thinking."

P. W. Bridgman: *The Nature of Physical Theory*

JACK OF EAGLES

chapter one

WHISPERS IN THE EARTH

Danny Caiden was reasonably sure that there was nothing wrong with him.

He had an average income, and enough education to handle the packaging section of a food-industry trade paper; even enough to write a poem or two on the side. Danny's poetry was certainly not very good yet, despite the interest the office aesthete took in it, but did serve as an outlet for the way he felt on good days and bad ones. He was a little under six feet, big-boned, with yellow hair, a friendly face with a nose that was slightly too large for it, and no obligations to anybody but himself.

He was like many of the people in the world he occupied, and he liked both the people and the world. On the rare days when he got sick of writing enthusiastically about the latest way of wrapping something basically inedible so that people would eat it, his stories became a little more acid than Henry Mall, the paper's senior editor, would allow anyone's stories but his own to be, and he had a beer or so before going back to his room-and-a-half on

11

13th Street. On the nights when he loved everybody and had Saturday or Sunday to look forward to, he had a lot of beers and slept until the next noon.

A normal guy, Danny thought. He lay on his bed and wriggled his stockinged toes in the yellow lamplight. He had no anxieties, no woman trouble, no compulsive political convictions. He didn't care who got elected this year or any year, and he didn't even have a cold.

But all the same, he was lying awake on his bed at three in the morning of a work-day, wondering why he had visions.

He turned the word over a few times. It was so remote from his thinking vocabulary that it probably never would sound right to him in any context; but it was the only word that gave him any handle at all for what had been happening to him. Actually, of course, what he had been having lately was voices—except that one didn't "have" voices, and besides, they weren't voices. They were just noises.

Noises that he heard twice, once inside his head, and once outside. Like double vision. Double audition? There might just be such a term, but it didn't sound right either.

He wriggled his toes and went over the day for at least the eighth time, trying to see what there was about it that he had missed so far which would allow him to label the experience in familiar terms.

Now then: He had come out of Childs after lunch, feeling a little too full, and had started to turn the corner to go back to the office. He remembered being in the middle of a step; remembered wishing that his other suit would get back from the cleaners; remembered wishing that lunch-hour could be followed by another hour for a cat-nap. He

12

remembered wondering whether or not the man from the orange-growers' association would confirm that idiotic report that had come in from *Food Chronicler's* Florida correspondent; and whether or not Mall would let Danny's caption for the bread-eating campaign picture go through. It wouldn't be fair, after all, to let the baking industry get away with bragging about putting back into bread half of the nutrients they'd taken out of it, without at least a mild dig . . .

Just around the corner, someone had screamed. There had been a shearing squeal of brakes and rubber. Then something metallic had hit something else. The impact was sudden and quickly over, almost as if a truck full of brass ingots had been run off a high building.

Then there were more screams, a dull boom, and . . . more screams, round and full and impossible to listen to. People were running.

Danny had not run. He had stopped abruptly, and put his back against the cool concrete flank of the building. A month ago—about that—he had been coming around this same corner, and had heard those same noises. He had run then.

But he'd found nothing around the corner but the usual agitated rivers of people trudging back from their lunch hours. No accident—no horrified crowd—nothing.

And so, this time, he had been afraid to go around the corner. The original illusion had gradually faded from his memory, but the fact brought it back. The exact, one-for-one correspondence of the sequences of sounds scared him. It was not the *déjà vu*, the momentary "recognition" of a place or event one actually has never seen before; Danny had experienced that as often as most normal persons, and knew that it was upsetting only because it was impossible to trace the false memory back to any real experience. But this—there was a real memory of all these shocking noises in Danny's mind, a memory he could place and date.

Which was why he was afraid to turn the corner; for he had no evidence yet that the second experience was any more real than the first one had been. Hard as it was to believe that his stable, basically untroubled mind was capable of handing him the first illusion, two such would be enough to upset the most phlegmatic of men.

People continued to run past Danny. He could not remember, then or now, *seeing* anybody running before; only hearing the sound of running. Something really had happened, then. Fried scallops clumping in his stomach, he went around the corner.

There had been an accident, all right. A cab, trying to beat a light, had hit an avenue bus amidships, and the gas tank of one of the two vehicles—it was hard to tell which —had burst. There was a pyre at the intersection. Carbonized bodies twitched feebly, some still managing to scream now and then. The mob was drawing in slowly, murmuring with fascination, but held off by the heat.

Danny, sick, had detoured, and stumbled his way to his elevator. He got off on the wrong floor, and was good for nothing for the rest of the afternoon.

It had been bad enough to have the sounds of that collision stored in his head—but for Danny, every one of those sounds had an echo. He had heard them all a month before they had happened.

He was bawled out twice by Mall for being sarcastic

14

about the merits of free enterprise, and failed dismally to respond to a gambit offered by the new redhead in the typing pool. He left the office ten minutes too early, and afterwards had taken aboard more than enough beer to put him back into a cheerful and uncritical state.

But still, at 3:00 A.M., Danny was sober, awake, and twitching his toes speculatively in the lamplight. For him, that collision had happened twice. Something had made him hear it before it had actually happened.

Now that he came to think of it, his mind had played him some tricks before—if they were tricks. At least, he could think of one odd gift, unimportant until now in his universe, for which he had no explanation, and which seemed to involve prediction of a sort: the thing he had always called "the finding trick."

He had been kidded about the finding trick for as long as he could remember, but it worked. It still did, or at least it had still been working the last time he had used it, in the middle of the winter just ended. Bill Emers had phoned him long-distance from Banff, drunker than Silenus, demanding to know where he'd misplaced his ski-wax.

Without bothering to think, Danny had said, "You put it on the right-hand corner of the mantel, but it's been dumped off somehow. It's probably in the scuttle with the fire-tools."

Which was where it was. Danny could still hear Emers chortling to his friends as he put the phone down, but he himself was bored with the finding trick, and more than bored by being forced to prove that he had it, every time some casual acquaintance wanted to liven up a party. He had never been to Banff, let alone to the lodge where Bill

15

Emers had been staying at the time; furthermore, he knew nothing about skiing except that it was a sport for people who, unlike Danny, didn't hate cold weather. He had simply spoken on impulse, as he always did when people asked him to find things they had lost.

And, he had always been right—every time.

So there it was. He took no stock in the supernatural; he was not much inclined to think even gods necessary, let alone spectres. But it was too late to ignore the fact that there was something strange about himself. Prophetic noises, and a long-range sensitivity to where things were . . .

Was that it, then? A sensitivity—a special ability to detect coming events, like a street wreck or the loss of some object like a can of ski-wax? It seemed useless, if that was what it was, but it was at least a start toward understanding. The daily papers often printed wide-eyed stories, especially in the mid-summer "silly season" when real news was suffering from the doldrums, about people who could pull off tricks that other people couldn't—women who glowed in the dark, girls who went floating unconscious out of their bedroom windows, little boys who attracted gushes of water or oil or even "flows" of mysterious rocks. As a newspaperman of a rather low grade, Danny had seen his fair share of such reports; the great press associations had odd ideas about what a paper dealing with food processing and packaging might like to print.

Danny got up on his elbows and reached for a cigarette. Maybe there was really a line there. It was probably foolish, but he could no longer just let these things happen to him. They were too hard on the nerves. And there might just be the chance that a special ability to guess right—not only about *where* things were, but *when* they would be there—could be brought under control, and used at will.

Danny didn't need too much imagination to think of ways to use a prophetic sense. It was time now to find out what he had and why he had it.

If he didn't find out pretty soon, there wouldn't be much left of his sanity. He wondered again if he were already slightly off his chump—the strange noises just the first signs of a crackup, not really related to outside events except through faulty memory or an irritated imagination . . .

But had he imagined Bill Emers' ski-wax, nestling there in the coal-scuttle among the fire-tools, or Bill's crow when he found it? That seemed unlikely. No, he'd have to go ahead on the assumption that he was still sane—find some of these people with weird talents—talk to them—run down whatever had been written about them, in news-papers- or anywhere else. He could start at the library. There had to be a lead somewhere.

Relaxed by the decision, he snubbed out the cigarette and began to loosen his tie. At the same instant, while he was still propped up on his elbows with his chin pointing at the ceiling, for the first time he heard voices.

He knew at once, without knowing how he knew, that they were not the voices of passersby on the street below. They were soundless; they were inside his head. And yet, at the same time, they came from below—a subterranean whispering, as if the very bedrock of the city had found a way to speak.

"There has been a Decision."

"*Yes. I have estanned the tension.*"

"*And I. The threshold has been crossed.*"

Soundless voices, whispering together, meaningless things. Danny felt the sweat coming out all over his body. The empty words had a cold tang of menace. And—they were about him. In the maddening way that he knew things these days, he could tell.

"*So many paths—may we never interfere?*"

"*No, my brother. All go to the same goal.*"

"*Let the finder beware.*"

"*Let him then beware. Let us wait.*"

"*Since the way is long, we must wait.*"

After that, there was a long inner silence. It took a while for Danny to realize that there was to be no more. It was as if he had heard so much only because it had touched upon him—as if the whisperers droned now of things incomprehensible and remote, though they still stood at his aching elbows. The words were still being spoken, but they were not for him.

Danny had the indefensible notion that he would have heard nothing even had he been imbedded in the rock with the whisperers, or they seated on the bed beside his pillow. Their lips would move meaninglessly for him, as if in an old silent film.

Or did the whisperers even have lips—or faces?

He put the question aside. The voices, for all their strange soundlessness, had been human. Their language had been English, except for that one strange word *estanning*, which might have been a word labelling the nature of their conversation itself. Danny was not ready to believe in ghosts—not yet.

18

He realized suddenly that he was utterly exhausted. Above and beyond the tiredness brought on by his night's vigil, he felt drained, half dead, as if the mere act of listening to that silent colloquy had been a feat of endurance. His heart thudded in a slow, leaden rhythm.

He fell back, trembling. One thing was sure—there was something abroad in the world that normal people like Danny Caiden had never suspected. Something that Danny Caiden was being driven to find, blindly, unwillingly, driven by an unmanageable irruption of wild talents. Something huge—unthinkable.

Let the finder beware . . .

chapter two

THE COMMITMENT

Except for a giddy tiredness, a sort of poisonous residue of last night's drained sensation, Danny felt much better by the next afternoon. It was one thing to be alone in a dark room, already overtired and upset, a prey to all sorts of dreams and delusions—and quite another to be thirty-four stories up in clear air, in bright sunlight, in one of the most modern office buildings in the whole city.

Prophetic sounds, whispering voices—the battering of Al Randall's typewriter at his back was rough on them. Every noisy impact of key on platen pushed them further into the fogs of unreality.

I'll have to start getting to bed earlier, Danny thought. I'm not a kid in college any longer. When it gets to the point where a simple street accident throws me for a loop, it's time to take steps. Hell, I saw worse things under worse conditions in the Army without going into any Section Eight spins afterwards. Still it wouldn't pay to invite it all to start adding up on me.

Joan Keyes, the senior editor's chief factotum, leaned

over his shoulder and tossed a sheaf of clippings and advertising agency releases onto his desk.

"Looks like a bad week," she said resignedly. "Nothing coming in so far but junk, and not much of that. There's a follow-up on your wienie-wrapper story in there."

"There is? You should give me big news like that in small doses. My heart isn't what it used to be."

Joan took off her pixie glasses and looked at Danny critically.

"Come to think of it," she said, "you do look a little wrung out today, Danny. Got a new girl? Or is the food business getting you down?"

"Sean would call it the Tantalus complex," Al said cheerfully, rearing back in his chair and putting on an intensely serious expression. Al came from a family of road-show actors, and his imitation of Sean Hennessy, the assistant news editor, was so exact that for a moment even his bushy brown moustache looked thinner and darker. "All day long we write about things to eat, and there's nothing to chew on in the office but the erasers on the pencils."

At this even Sean grinned; Danny was a notorious pencil-biter.

"I didn't get much sleep last night," Danny said. It made him uneasy again to have to talk about it, as if talking about it somehow made it a little more real once more. "That accident yesterday made me nervous, and then I had funny dreams."

"Dreams?" said Sean, pricking up his ears. As Al had indicated, Sean was something of a parlor Freudian, given to spot analyses of everyone he met; he had once declared

21

Pat Rickey, the big boss, to be an "oral personality." "What kind of dreams?"

"He dreamt he was Drew Pearson," an angry voice snapped from the door. A prickly lump in his throat, Danny looked over his shoulder.

The voice belonged to Rickey, who in addition to being officially The editor of all eight trade papers put out by the Delta Publishing Company, was also one of the firm's few owners. It was only the second time he'd been in the *Food Chronicler's* editorial cubby since Danny had been working there. In one hand he shook a copy of the *Chronicler*, crumpled into a rough tube. Danny couldn't see which issue it was.

Rickey said, "Where's Mall?"

"He's talking to Mr. Masciarelli in Accounting," Joan said. "Is something wrong, Mr. Rickey?"

"Something wrong! I've got a twenty-four EOM insertion advertiser on my wire, burning hot and ready to cancel, that's all."

Rickey jerked Joan's extension from its crutch and growled into it.

Joan looked inquiringly at Danny. He had nothing to offer but a miserable shrug.

Almost before Rickey put the phone down, Mall, the senior editor, was in the office, looking faintly green and stuttering slightly with excitement. Mall had never quite got over his first fear of being fired, though he had been with the firm eighteen years and drew ten thousand a year plus profit-sharing.

"Now let's get to the bottom of this," Rickey said grimly. "Your by-line is on this story, Caiden. According to you,

22

International Wheat is due to be hit for price-fixing this week. International is going to cancel its contract with us. It may also sue us for libel, and small wonder. Mall, how did this get past you?"

Mall turned a little greener.

"That's the issue that came out last week?" he said. "I was at the Canners' Convention during m-most of the time when it was b-being put together. Joan was in charge."

Joan looked at the editor, her glance darting over the tops of her glasses like a schoolteacher pinning down an unmannerly boy.

"That's right," she said primly. "I saw the story, and passed the statement. Why shouldn't I have? Danny had no reason to make up a thing like that."

"I don't know," Mall said. "He's like m-most of the rest of you—thinks the day's wasted if he c-can't be sarcastic about big business at least once. I'd like just once to get s-somebody in here who doesn't think the food business should be c-conducted at the United Nations level."

Joan looked more like a schoolteacher than ever.

"Don't be ridiculous, Henry," she said. "You'd think price-fixing was Danny's personal invention, to hear you talk. There's been an indictment a week for it, ever since the multiple-basing-point decision was handed down."

"What kills me," Rickey said, "is that there was no need to bring the subject up in a packaging story at all—and if it's actually true, it belongs in a five-column banner across page one. Instead, it's just dropped in here, as if it were common knowledge. Listen: 'One probable result of general adoption of the new machinery will be increased conservation of American-Egyptian wheat, which is ex-

23

pected to be in short supply after the price-fixing indictment against the International Wheat Corp. is filed. At
last reports, the indictment was still due Sept. 2nd.' In
other words, this Friday!"

"That's ridiculous," Mall said.

"Of course it's ridiculous. My only chance to keep the
Wheat ads in the book is to convince the agency that anybody who happens to spot the buried reference will automatically discount it as hogwash. Hell, I've even had a
call from the SEC, wanting to know who over here was
responsible for such nonsense!"

"Why not get the source material out of the files?" Al
suggested practically. "If it says International was due to
be indicted, Danny was within his rights in reporting it.
The food business is a big industry—I'm always running
across things that make my hair stand on end that turn out
to be common knowledge. I'll never forget my first encounter with the Danville decision, for instance."

"It'd be no less libelous legally for being the truth,"
Rickey muttered; but he seemed to be willing enough to
look at the evidence.

Danny tried to remember what had happened to the
source material on the story. The "files" to which Al had
referred were actually a set of bins, into which dead releases, clippings, and stories from field correspondents
were thrown after an issue was put to bed, stuffed in kraft
envelops bearing the date of the issue in question. As soon
as a bin was six months dead, its contents were baled and
sold to be re-pulped.

As far as Danny could remember, the original of the
story—a release, with pictures, one of which he had used,

24

from the Packaging Machinery Institute—hadn't been binned. He'd put it in his bottom desk drawer, along with the carbon of his story, to await a possible three-em add—a paragraph to be added to the *Chronicler's* account, under a three-em dash, at the last minute, should the actual indictment come through earlier than expected.

As he pawed through the papers in the drawer, he felt a sick certainty that the release wouldn't justify him. He hadn't made the part of the story that had upset Rickey out of whole cloth, but out of absolute certainty—the kind of certainty Rickey had accurately ticketed as a feeling of "common knowledge."

What if that "certainty" had been just another wild, uncontrollable phantasm, unbackable by anything in the source files? If Mall didn't know about the indictment, it was a cinch that it was *not* common knowledge, even among experts.

"Here it is," he said shakily. He was afraid to look at it. He passed it to Sean, who was closest. Sean immediately began to read it with unabashed curiosity, but Rickey jerked it from his hands.

Rickey devoured the mimeographed sheets slowly, line by line, word by word, his eyes bulging gluttonously, mumbling key phrases under his breath. Danny began to understand better what Sean meant by an "oral" personality. Rickey took in that pompously unimportant announcement as if he were a cannibal and it were a fat missionary. At the end, he emitted a sigh of fierce repletion.

"Not a word," he said. "Not one single damned word. Anything to say, Caiden?"

Danny swallowed. "The week isn't over yet," he said.

25

"They'll be hit on or before Friday—on nine counts, price-fixing being one, all under the 'discriminatory sales practices' provisions of the Robinson-Patman Act."

It was Joan who actually asked the lethal question, but it might just as well have been anyone in the tense little office. She said:

"Danny, how do you know?"

All five of them looked at him: Joan, Al and Sean with hope, Mall with indifference, Rickey with a sort of moral indignation.

Danny's tired brain raced, but somehow the clutch wasn't in. He knew that he knew. International Wheat would get its indictment tomorrow or Friday. It was the original leadpipe cinch.

But he did not know how he knew.

The silence ran out like sand. Rickey said:

"All right, Caiden. Pick up your check as you leave."

chapter three

~~~~~~

ENTER DR. FREUD

Danny packed up his property in complete silence—necessarily, because Rickey remained in the cubby to see to it that he left the premises promptly. Joan and Al fiddled aimlessly with pencils, and would not look at each other, or at Danny. Sean ripped the long yellow sheet of copy paper out of his typewriter, collapsed the typewriter into the desk and glared belligerently at Mall.

Mall stood up under Sean's Irish indignation for a moment, then sat down at his own desk, pulled his typewriter stand between himself and the rest of the office, and ostentatiously began to type. His machine was a "noiseless," but it seemed inordinately loud.

Danny took a manila envelope from the supply shelf and dumped his papers and his 25¢ dictionary into it. He was beginning to be angry. In the middle drawer of what had been his desk he found a pica rule and the remains of a box of soft blue pencils, all strictly the property of Delta Publishing Co., and dropped them in too.

Rickey said nothing. He waited until Danny had closed

the flap on the envelop, sprung the metal clasp, and had begun to take his topcoat off the hanger snubbed over the top of the open door of the cubby. Then he left, trailing a faint aroma of executive satisfaction.

Mall continued to type. Sean got up.

"Going my way, Danny?" he said.

Mall stopped typing abruptly. "Did you get that Coffee Bureau story, Hennessy?" he said. His eyes were directed toward a spot about two feet over Sean's left shoulder.

"Yes," Sean said. "I got it. I have a place to put it, too, if you're interested. Bean by bean, so to speak."

Danny plucked at Sean's sleeve. "Don't," he said. "It's all over now, anyhow. It isn't your fight, Sean. There's more to it than you can see."

"I don't give a damn. I'm sick of trying to be subservient, especially on *my* salary. Mall palls on me, all of a sudden. He's too timid to stand up for his own staff. What are you writing, pall Mall? An editorial?"

"I—" Mall said.

"Full of resounding clichés—blow hot, blow cold, say nothing, eh?" Sean said. His young face, as dark and beardless as a Spaniard's, was full of pleasure. "What is it now— The Speech about free enterprise? It couldn't be anything about food. You don't know anything about food. You live on plaster, like a silverfish—but attractively packaged, of course."

"You're fired," Mall said, looking back to his typewriter. "Get out. Both of you."

Sean chuckled. He smiled at Danny. "Isn't he quick?" he said. "You only have to hit him four times, and he begins to wonder if he's uncomfortable. Of course he won't

28

know he's uncomfortable until Rickey tells him he is. Let's go have a drink."

It was hard not to be delighted by Sean's jubilant support. But Sean seemed to have spent his whole life in the windy sunlit air thirty-four stories above the street. He might easily have just tossed up his job in defense of madness.

Sean was quiet in the elevator, and remained so until the two ex-editors were settled in a booth in the nearest bar. But he looked gleeful all the way.

He settled himself into the cushions and signaled for a waiter. "Been wanting to do that for three years," he said suddenly. "Glad you gave me the excuse—two beers, junior —or I might never have done it. Somehow I think I was afraid to do it on my own. So—that's that."

"That is definitely that," Danny agreed solemnly. "I've never seen anything that-er. What are you going to do, Sean? Any plans?"

"I'm crawling with plans. What else have I had to daydream about? My trouble is that I'm hard put to it to make a choice among them. Maybe now I can start going to school in the daytime, and use my nights for something constructive, like the cultivation of a small patch of blondes. I might even be able to get my degree before the war breaks out—not that I'll have any use for it then. I wouldn't mind, I suppose. Do you know, Danny, I really loved combat? First time in my life I ever felt like somebody. What's your trouble, Danny?"

The question fell so unexpectedly and with such little apparent significance into the midst of Sean's chatter that Danny found himself answering without the slightest forethought. Maybe Sean really ought to be a psychoanalyst after all, Danny thought, listening to his own innocent answer winding out of him. He obviously had a real gift for luring people into talking about the theoretically unmentionable.

Yet, once launched, Danny could see no reason still why he should not tell Sean the story. Sean was in his fix now, and perhaps deserved to know something about the idiot cause for which he had stood up.

The beer helped. Hesitantly, it all came out—the noises, the finding trick, the flash of certainty that had gotten them both fired.

Somehow, though, he knew it was important not to mention the voices. Partly, it was important because it would worry Sean, make him think perhaps that Danny was off his rocker in some obvious, demonstrable way. That was a demonstration Danny didn't care to face—not just yet. And, partly, because, well, because he knew the voices were important—knew it with as strong a conviction as he knew that International Wheat would be indicted tomorrow or Friday.

"I think there've been some other examples, but I can't remember them all," he wound up. "There's a lot of stuff in the background that isn't at all definitive; it helps me to build up a case for myself, but nobody else could accept it as evidence for anything at all."

"You and your tight sphincter," Sean said. "Isn't what you've told me already disorganized enough? Out with it."

"Well, I was usually called a 'good guesser' when I was a kid. And—I hadn't thought of this before at all, but it does seem to fit—the few times I got to the movies in the

Bingo days, or bought tickets for some raffle or drawing, I always got something. Not always first prize, I don't mean that, but I did always come home with some trinket or other.

"Once, during a giveaway stunt in a theater, when I was nine, I won a coffee pot. The guy on the stage made some crack about Boy Scouts and camping trips, because I was wearing khaki shorts and a khaki shirt. I wouldn't be caught dead in shorts now, let me tell you.

"And once I won a pig. An honest-to-god live pig, in a Thanksgiving drawing. I wanted to keep it for a pet. The theater had had it out in the lobby in a small pen, it was clean and quite small, about the size of a mongrel dog, or maybe a little smaller. But my parents wouldn't let me. They had it butchered and we ate it on Thanksgiving. My parents didn't like it—said it was too young to have any flavor—and it made me mad that they'd gone and had it killed, and then complained afterwards."

Sean grinned and wiped beer foam off his narrow meticulous moustache.

"But you ate it too, without a qualm, didn't you, Danny?" he said. "You were going to have that pig, one way or another. You're the perfect anal personality—possessive, griping. My God, but you're normal."

"What I've been telling you is normal?" Danny said, a little irritated.

"Well, it's expectable, anyhow. First of all, let's talk about your 'wild-talents' theory. I won't surprise you if I say that I don't take much stock in it, Danny. It's ingenious, but it breaks down.

"What kind of imaginable talent, wild or otherwise,

31

could take the proper number out of a hat without seeing it—and at the same time affect the numbers everybody else took out of the hat, thoroughly enough to make the initial number the inevitable winner? Anybody who could control chance that far would be able to slow up horses, or push the stock market around, without even stopping to think."

"Um," Danny said. "Yeah. I hadn't thought of that."

"What interests me," Sean said, "is a great howling gap in your story about how you find things. What happened to this guy Bill Emers, for instance?"

Danny frowned. "Why, I never did see him again," he said. "He was killed at Banff that winter. Went tail over teacup off a ski-jump, and broke his spine in two places. I suppose he was drunk—he was drunk most of the time."

"Aha!" Sean pounced upon the answer. "But you didn't have any premonition of this? Didn't have any premonitory noises, or other sensations that you could interpret as predicting his death?"

"No-o-o-o. That kind of thing hasn't been happening to me frequently, though, until lately, as I said."

"Of course it hasn't. It's never even occurred to you, consciously, that Bill Emers undoubtedly died the same day that you found his ski-wax for him!"

"That's just an assumption."

"The hell it is. Your mind wouldn't be behaving this way if it didn't know it to be a fact. I dare you to check the date, Danny. Or, no, I don't; it wouldn't be therapeutic unless you had some guidance from an analyst. But your unconscious plainly suspects it—and blames itself! Accidentally you made a perfectly logical guess about the ski-

32

wax—I think I'd have made a very similar guess under those circumstances. But the results—

"When you heard of Bill's death, you felt guilty. Naturally. You found him his ski-wax: he went skiing: he died. Since your rational mind told you that you weren't guilty, and your unconscious told you that you were, you began to have compensatory symptoms. Your mind was trying to resolve a dilemma. And after the symptoms got disturbing enough, you concocted this 'wild talents' theory to explain them. The real explanation was much too deeply buried, and much too disturbing, for you to reach it by yourself."

Sean shoved his empty glass out to the edge of the table and tapped twice.

"Danny, to put it bluntly, you knew—subconsciously—that if you hadn't found Bill Emers his ski-wax, he probably wouldn't have tried to make a jump while drunk. Not that day, anyhow. You've been blaming yourself ever since.

"But you're not to blame. You didn't get him drunk; you weren't responsible for his love of drinking; and you couldn't have stopped him from killing himself eventually. As soon as that sinks in, Danny, I think your troubles will be about over."

The waiter took away the foam-etched glasses, filled them again and returned them while Danny thought about it. Sean looked as warily self-contained as a cat who has just caught a big moth—the victim still fluttering frantically, but available for the kill at pleasure.

Finally Danny said, "That's good, Sean. I wish I could swallow it. It makes more sense than my theory. But what bothers me is, why should I care about Bill Emers? I

c   33 hardly knew him. He just called me for a gag—he'd heard rumors about my finding trick."

"Resentment," Sean said. "Nobody likes to be the butt of a joke. When you heard that he'd been killed, your resentment seemed to you like a good motive for murder."

"To quote the late Henry Mall, that's ridiculous."

"What of it? Believe me, Danny, the unconscious isn't rational, it has no sense of humor—and it *never* forgets. It can make you feel to blame for all kinds of fantastic things—things you wouldn't even think of doing with the top of your mind."

"Okay," Danny said. "But this still doesn't explain why I had the reputation for the finding trick in the first place. Everybody I used to know in college came to me to ask where to find things—from a misplaced slide rule all the way to a wallet with fifty-eight bucks in it. I told 'em where to look, and I was always right. Otherwise they'd have stopped coming to me."

Sean didn't appear to be in the least disturbed. "Coincidence," he said, dipping his nose appreciatively into his beer. "People have an absurd faith in the limited principles of chance. Mathematically it's perfectly possible for coincidences to happen in indefinitely long chains."

"But they don't, all the same."

"But they do," Sean said. He pointed a long, slender finger at Danny. "They happen all the time. Why shouldn't they? In an infinity of time, anything can happen, regardless of its apparent absurdity. Water can freeze on a fire, light can go to its source instead of away from it, things can fall up—such things can happen repeatedly, and to hell with whether or not they violate chance. The 'law' of chance is just a local ordinance. We have a whole school of scholarly nincompoops who keep tabs on repeated coincidences—with cards and dice and 'predictions' and everything else under the sun."

"You must mean the parapsychologists at the university. I was asked to be a guinea-pig of theirs, one year."

"Yes, them. When they get enough coincidences written down—about dice, say—they claim that the man throwing the dice exerts some occult influence on them! Shooting craps on a mystic blanket! That's just a professorial version of your 'wild talents' theory, except that *those* birds ought to know better.

"Danny, you're just a victim of super-coincidence. You're in a bad psychological situation because of your guilt feelings over your drunken skier. As it happens, at the same time you're involved in what a mathematician would call a random chain, a chain of improbabilities *which all the same are real*, and that gives you superficially good methods for rationalizing your troubles."

It sounded reasonable, though where a minor trade-paper editor like Sean had picked up all this high-powered information was difficult to fathom. Danny said, "I guess you're right, Sean. Got any recommendations?"

"I'm no analyst," Sean said. "If you have the dough, see a good one. But in the meantime, try to realize that you're just feeling guilty about Bill's death; and that, realistically, you're not responsible for it. If you don't manage to convince yourself of that—well, sooner or later the random chain is going to break on you, and you'll have to concoct some other rationalization to explain away the truth. Your

35

next rationalization is a cinch to be twice as nutty as your present one. They always are."

"I sort of thought I might go nuts over this business," Danny said. He got up. He had seen Sean order no more than two rounds, but somehow he was almost tight.

Jeepers—this thing really does have me down. Two-beer Caiden. What did Bill Emers look like, anyhow? I can't even remember that much.

"Goodbye," he said. "Thanks, Sean."

He went out, walking carefully.

chapter four

THE CLOUDED CRYSTAL BALL

The golden curtain thrown across the door of the bar was only sunlight, but he was almost afraid to walk through it. Normality seemed very shaky to him.

But the world outside was the same world into which he had emerged after being fired. Traffic droned along the asphalt. Pedestrians swung past him, heads slightly lowered, intent upon their business. High overhead among the pinnacles of the buildings a lone pontoon plane cruised, watching the harbor for the Port Authority. It was all very normal.

How normal can you get?

Sean had said, "My God, but you're normal." But he had meant, *My God, you're neurotic.* In Sean's world, no other situation was "normal."

Here, at least, Danny had one measure of his suddenly suspect normality. He had come to Delta Publishing Company as a job-trainee under the GI Bill. The tests given him by the Veterans Administration to determine his eligibility had been incredibly, and it had seemed to him unnecessarily exhaustive, and they had included a whole series of psychological tests—Sanford-Binet, the Minnesota Multiphasic, all three California Tests, Allport-Vernon, Wechsler-Belvue, Pintner, Bernreuter, Otis, Rorschach, Szondi —the works. Most of them had seemed so far afield from any strain editing the packaging page of a food paper might have put upon him as to make him wonder why he hadn't also been required to get Security clearance.

Nor had he been very happy with the results. "You're normal," the interviewer had told him. "Oh, there's just a slight tendency toward hypochondria, but well within the safe limits. I wouldn't mention it at all if it weren't for the way your profile sticks so close to the mean on all other elements. Don't look so uncomfortable, Mr. Caiden; you should congratulate yourself. People with IQs as high as yours usually have psychological profiles as ragged as the blade of a rusty ripsaw. I know it's fashionable to be neurotic, but you'll never make the grade, Mr. Caiden. You're abnormally normal, if you'll forgive me the oxymoron."

That had been two years ago. Now, if Danny could believe Sean, he was far gone; not merely a neurotic, but perilously near being an out-and-out psychotic.

It simply couldn't have happened that fast. Furthermore, Danny was not entirely ignorant of Freud; few college graduates are. Even without Sean's more detailed interest in Freudianism, Danny remembered well Freud's principle dictum: *No neurosis is possible without an abnormal sexual life.*

Danny didn't need any recourse to Kinsey to tell him

that in this area, too, he was still—normal; pleasantly, dully normal.

He smiled mirthlessly at his normal self. All right, Caiden, then you've got to be a prophet. Get over your shock; you made yourself promises about what you'd do if you turned out to have a real prophetic sense. You don't turn out to have much else. Are you going to follow through?

The question, of course, was rhetorical. Danny knew of no other way to keep himself eating. He had no talent for writing fiction—whatever Pat Rickey might even now be saying to the contrary notwithstanding—and trade editorial jobs, the only kind for which he was equipped, were tighter this year than they had ever been before. His one chance was to sink his few cents in a fantasm.

Shrugging, he crossed the street. He certainly had had no plans to approach the skyscraper housing Delta Publishing again except by accident. Of course, his bank was on the ground floor of the building—Delta did its payroll banking there, and so it had saved him troublesome sidetrips, and the bother of having to identify himself and his paychecks, to stow his small savings cheek to cheek with his ex-bosses' hoard—but since it was only a savings account, he had planned simply to leave it alone until he was desperate.

Well, he was desperate now, though in an unanticipated meaning of the word. He went to one of the glass-topped desks which surrounded each of the pillars inside the bank and took his pass book out of his wallet.

He was surprised to find that he had close to two thousand dollars in his account; he would have guessed it at

39

less than half that. Well, that should certainly be ample. There was a good deal to be said for being a bachelor.

But the size of the sum set his mind to whirling furiously again, even while he was filling out the withdrawal ticket. Savings as comfortable as that would provide an unanticipated cushion for job-hunting—

No, it wouldn't do. Savings dollars spent these days on daily living were about 64% wasted, prices being as wildly inflated as they were. A dollar had to make money to retard its own diminishing value. To waste it hunting virtually non-existent trade editorial jobs would be stupid, when the possibility existed that it could be invested in a high-return enterprise.

It was Danny's intuition that there was no higher-return investment than precognition—if it paid off at all.

He withdrew the money, to the obvious prim disapproval of the teller—what stake could *he* have in it, anyhow?— and left the building once more, and, he hoped, forever.

A subway took him to the city's financial district, and an elevator took him up to the brokerage firm which had been the object of a field trip for Danny's Economics class during his last year in college.

The junior partner of the firm, trained to remember the most insignificant face and name against the possible development that there should be money attached to it, received him with apparent pleasure.

"I want to try a few small transactions," Danny said steadily. "Studying, you understand. I've some money to spare, and I think actually entering it on the market would be valuable laboratory experience for me."

"Possibly even profitable," the broker said. "We're tak-
40

ing a special interest in small investors these days, because capital's needed pretty badly. So much is being soaked up by defense industries. Let me see—you're interested in the food business, as I remember; I can offer you some shares in a frozen food subsidiary of one of the major companies—quite sound, and likely to be going up almost indefinitely."

"No, I'm not interested in that kind of thing; on a long-term investment I'd stick to debentures or a savings-and-loan plan, anyhow. That would make me money in the long run, but it wouldn't teach me anything I didn't already know. What I want to do is speculate."

The broker smiled ruefully. "Speculate?" he said. "No sewers where you live? The market is tossing like a drunken madman this week. You couldn't have picked a worse time. Personally, Mr. Caiden, I'd advise you just to throw your money off the back of a truck. It's simpler; less mental agony."

"I've no personal interest in the money," Danny insisted. "Win or lose, I want to see what happens and how it happens."

"All right. We'll do our best for you. What would you like us to do?"

"Is it too late to sell Wheat short?"

The broker leaned back in his chair with a patronizing smile. "Sell it short! My lord, man, you'll lose your pants. Wheat's going up like a rocket, thanks to the war scare. Or do you want to get in on futures? If so, you're in the wrong place; we don't handle commodities here, just stocks."

"No, I mean stock in International Wheat, as a corporation. I've no interest in futures. Give me an option on ten shares at 16. You should find plenty of takers. Close with the first one, and sell when it hits 16 on the downgrade."

"I suppose that you know 16 stands for sixteen hundred dollars—it hasn't hit that on the *up*-grade yet. Oh, well, don't remind me again that your purpose is scientific. I'm not used to being so objective. Any special time to be watchful?"

Danny knew that the broker secretly considered him to be an idiot, but he kept his patience. After all, the broker quite probably was right. "Friday, I should say, but it could break tomorrow."

"All right," the broker said. "Normally, I'd have to ask you for security, as I'm sure you know, but I can't see any likelihood that the SEC could object to this kind of deal. If it works, of course, it'll be a killer, but I'll tell you frankly that it won't. Anyhow I'll play it your way."

"What's the damage?"

"Why, 10%—sixteen hundred, the same as you'd pay for one share if you were actually buying it. But you'd better make it a flat two thousand, because you'll need margin if we're to bail you out."

"You won't need to," Danny said. He handed a certified check for just $1600 across the desk. The broker put it in his middle desk drawer without looking at it, shrugged, and wrote Danny a receipt for the same amount.

"Do you know what's going to happen if it does work out the way you predict?"

Danny shook his head.

"Just pray you don't find out," the broker said. "If you're right, you'll find that there's worse things than losing
42

your pants. Speculation isn't what it used to be before the government regulations came in; a sudden fortune these days is usually—uh, embarrassing." He looked down at his note-pad. "Now, if that's all for the moment—"

"That," Danny said, "is just the beginning."

Which it was. Sean had first put the idea of playing the market into his head; and Sean also had mentioned horses.

While his courage and his money still lasted, Danny located a bookie joint. Theoretically they were illegal in the city, and scarce to boot since the heyday of the Kefauver Quiz; but actually they were still seldom bothered and were easy to find. When in doubt, one could always ask a hackie.

Danny settled himself comfortably in a corner booth with a beer and a copy of the day's Racing Form. Something about him—perhaps it was the moderately clean shirt—tipped off the regular customers. Within five minutes he was approached by as many touts, all with tips directly out of the feedbag for a very small fee.

Danny waved them off. This operation, like the Wheat speculation, was going to be run strictly by feel, without the slightest heed to acknowledged authorities, reputable or otherwise. He was accepting no information, no matter how good it seemed, which did not come to him out of his own head.

He placed his bets, and waited.

It took only two hours to make his nerves as jumpy and his shirt as wilted as those of the oldest habitué. At first he had lunged halfway out of his booth every time the bar's phone rang. Now he just flinched a little and

43

clenched his teeth. It might have been less harrowing had the bar had its radio tuned to the crummy New Jersey station which existed to follow the races, but Kefauver's minions had driven that station back into harmless commercial ballads and macaroni commercials.

After a moment's telephone muttering, a waiter in a filthy apron put another beer, mostly head, in front of Danny.

"You sure ain't pickin' 'em today, bub," he said kindly. "Why don't you give over and go back home? Joe'll forgive you."

Danny smiled feebly. "I picked a caboose again, eh? Well, we'll give it one more turn. Let's make it—um—ten to win on High Heart in the next."

"Your funeral. I'll tell Joe."

The waiter went away. Danny nursed the beer, which was warm, and thumbed the money in his jacket pocket. There had still been a fair wad of it, about $300, when he had left the broker's office. Now there were three bills and a handful of change. The precognitive sense had definitely cut out of operation. Or else it was playing hooky at some other racetrack altogether.

Danny wondered suddenly if it were gone for good. He realized that his head was aching, sharply.

The phone rang. Danny's head rang with it.

"High Heart wins," the waiter said, appearing magically with a full glass of beer, beaded with cold and minus the Coney Island head. "Three to one. Mebbe your luck's turned."

"Tell Joe to put the whole wad on Double Trouble to place."

44

"Why don't you just take your winnin's?" the waiter said. "Joe don't mind. He's honest when he has a good day, which is mostly, anyhow."

"Double Trouble to place," Danny snapped. The headache was beginning to get much worse.

"All right, all right." The waiter scuffed surly feet back toward the bar. Danny let the beer sit where it was and nursed his head instead. The pain was localizing now, a tiny, white-hot thread deep inside his skull. He was beginning to see garish pinwheels.

"Double Trouble places," the waiter said. Danny had not heard the phone ring. He blinked, his eyes watering. "I will keep my big yap shut, mister. What'll it be?"

Danny looked at the form. It was hard even to see the printing, let alone make out what it said. He tried to concentrate.

Abruptly, the headache stopped. The sudden cessation of pain was almost as dizzying as the pain itself.

"Ugh," he said involuntarily.

"Huh?"

"Sorry—my head hurts—hurt. I'll take Pally, to win."

The waiter opened his mouth, seemed to remember his promise, and shut it again. Danny looked at the beer, then pushed it away. The after-effects of the headache were still making him a little seasick. He remembered the sensation of deadly fatigue which had struck him down at the end of last night, after he had overheard—*estanned?*— the strange whispering.

Evidently there were plenty of growing pains connected with the development of these wild talents.

The phone rang, and Danny felt himself stiffening.

45

If this one paid off, he told himself, he'd go home and take himself a rest. Already, two years seemed to have passed since last night.

The waiter was standing silently beside the table, his hands linked across his belly under the apron.

"Well?"

"Flash in the pan," the waiter said. "Joe says he wants you to quit. That'll be ten bucks for the beers."

"Ten bucks!"

"Just like I said, Mister."

On second thought, it wasn't surprising. The place was illegal anyhow. The price of the beers probably covered the overhead—the cost of keeping the police looking the other way. Everything was overpriced nowadays, even headaches. He threw his last tenspot on the table and stumbled out.

Precognition had blown a fuse.

chapter five

THE MEDIUM AND THE TELEPHONE

The disastrous conclusion of the wild move left Danny floundering in the worst tangle of loose ends he could remember. There was nothing for him to do now but wait for Friday to come around. If the International Wheat affair paid off in kind with the horse-playing, Danny would just as soon have Friday take its time.

The sunlight poured almost horizontally between the close-set, massive buildings of the financial district. Anonymous collars zigzagged homeward in a welter of homburgs. The business day was over. Danny wondered how many of the swinging briefcases, like his, had never contained anything but the day's lunch.

Down by the river and the freight wharves, the Solid Merit thinned out a little—just enough to admit a spur of the moribund El, a few bars and soda fountains, a few tiny shops. Danny wandered, drifting, in his own personal fog of confusion that no sun could penetrate.

He was glumly amused to find two narrow, paired windows on the street under the El that were full of

47

grimy dream-books, out-of-date astrology magazines, and pamphlets on phrenology. The little shop had once been an outlet of the A & P, as the big red and gold sign over it attested; but while it was waiting for a new lessee, it had evidently taken in a family of gypsies.

On the last count, however, he discovered that he was wrong. The inside of the store was not decorated with the gaudily-dyed cheesecloth drapes and curtains that gypsies ordinarily put up in such an establishment. And on the door he found a neat sign:

Mme. Zaza
Occultist & Medium

And then he knew, quite suddenly, that he was going to go in and talk to the medium.

Well—why not? She might be—was almost certainly—a faker; but he was no less cast out onto the marches of sanity than she. It might be that her talents were as real—and as undependable—as his.

That undependability would answer a good many questions about the social status of mediums. If one's sense of prophecy were in a vestigial or a highly undeveloped stage, it would be easy to misinterpret the results, and easiest to misinterpret them in terms of traditional supernaturalism. And on the other hand, if that were so, a really expert medium might well have some answers for Danny.

He went in. There was nothing in the front room but two chairs and a table, and a window, with dirty flowered chintz drapes, which gave on an airshaft. The table might once have been intended to be American Colonial, but if so, someone had attempted to reconvert it to Chinese Modern with a blunt penknife. It was bare, as was the floor. The air was musty with the odor of departed vegetables. The doorway at the back, which had once led to the A & P's stockroom, was curtained with a moth-raddled Axminster rug.

A moment after Danny had closed the front door, the rug was moved aside, and a girl came out. She was small and dark, with—after all—what seemed to be a trace of the gypsy, or at least of the Slav in her. She was conventionally dressed in a dark tailored suit whose severity, cut to a cheap dressmaker's ideas of classic simplicity, was absurdly schoolmarmish over the intensity of curves of which she was composed.

The girl seemed to burn through her clothes toward him. She was perhaps not quite pretty, and it was obvious that by the time she had passed 25, unless she took care, she would have thickened into something resembling a scale model of a subway kiosk. But Danny did not care. His first girl had been a Pole, and the type had always seemed to him to contain everything exquisite. For the moment, he had totally forgotten his madness, and the things that made it important. He simply stood and looked.

The girl looked back. Her eyes burned sullenly, and her mouth was set in an expression of contempt that should have seemed to Danny jarringly incongruous on so young a face. To another observer, also, the girl would have looked decidedly cheap. All these things Danny noted, but without taking any interest in them. The glossy, straight-seamed, muted decorum of Joan Keyes and quite a few other whited sepulchres he had met in publishers'

offices and advertising agencies had set him up for someone dark and disorderly and unsanctionable.

"What can I do for you?"

The voice was husky almost to harshness, not naturally
deep, but blurred as if forced to speak just after a serious
quarrel. Danny said:

"Are hmn. Are you Mme. Zaza?"

The girl smiled angrily. When she smiled, she was most
abruptly and violently beautiful. "No," she said. She
scanned Danny frankly from crown to toes. Then she
shrugged and turned away. "I'll fetch her."

She went back inside again. Danny tried to marshal
his thoughts, but they were aswim in the tide of an emotion he had not suffered for years. When he discovered
that there were great droplets of sweat along his forehead,
standing on his scalp under his hair, and running down
his cheeks past his ears, it did not even occur to him to
blame wild talents, or their exhaustion.

After a while the rug was pulled aside again. The girl
at 45 came out—squat, dowdy, seamed, hung with flashy
unfittable cloth in every possible mismatching of color,
and mustached and noticeably dirty to boot. A gypsy, all
right—in the last stages of civilization.

"Mme. Zaza?"

"Yes," she said. "Please come in."

Beyond the rug, there was a large room with dull scarlet
hangings, and in the center a card table supporting a glass
ball. The girl stood at the back of the room, not looking
at Danny. A thing like a tin fish-horn hung overhead, between Danny and the girl above the table, suspended
by two obvious black threads.

"You seek to know the future?" the medium said in a throaty voice. "Sit there."

"Not exactly. What I think I want is professional advice. I'm in trouble."

"My help is for all Lost Ones," the woman intoned smoothly. "Let the Forces That Be assume your burdens. Sit there, please. What are your troubles?"

"Well, I've had some experiences lately that made me think I might be—I guess I'll have to call it psychic."

The girl sniffed audibly. The medium shot her a glance that looked to be composed of the purest poison. The girl shrugged and went out, by what Danny had taken to be the door to the toilet.

"Please be seated," the medium said. "Thank you. Your trouble is not as secret or as unusual as you may think, I am told. All seek wisdom, but not all find it."

"Yes I know—that is so," Danny could not resist interjecting. The medium's purportedly ancient wisdom, however, did not seem to include Gilbert & Sullivan.

"There are those whose Karma seeks the True Wisdom and finds it. There are those also whose Will to Nirvana has become trapped in the Wheel. For these Trapped Ones, a Guru is needful—as needful as Must to Will."

"I don't seem to be following you," Danny said.

"Listen and understand," said Mme. Zaza. She made passes over the crystal globe, as if she were attempting to turn a rowboat around. The interior of the globe promptly swirled with smoke.

"Those whose gift it is," she said, "to speak a little with the Great Outside know that man has nine souls, even as the Egyptian Mages whispered long ago. Of these,

51

the least important is the Shadow. The most important is the Ka, which lives after the body on the far side of time. When the stars are propitious, it is possible to summon the Ka—"

The trumpet gave a premonitory squawk, as if clearing its throat.

"Look," Danny said, a little desperately. "Would you mind if I asked the questions? I'm not interested in talking with anybody's Ka. I can see the future a little myself, and sometimes some—other things that I don't understand. I want to know how to control it and anything else I might find myself able to do. Isn't that simple enough?"

The woman lifted her eyes raptly. "It is a great gift, to have the Sight," she said. "It makes one very humble. But it takes much practice to become an Adept."

"*That* I don't doubt. What kind of practise? Mental exercises? How do you—"

"Not *mental* exercises, young man. Shun the cold intellect vaulted by the materialistic West." (Danny was reasonably sure she meant "vaunted;" but it was her first such slip that he had detected. Wherever she had picked up her thumping phrases, she had perfected them with great care.) "What matters is the soul, or rather, the Oversoul—the Ka. It must be sent from the body into the Great Outside, to learn there whatever it can learn. If the spirits are willing, it will return with great riches."

"Sent out? In a trance?"

"That is one way. There are others. These are not things to be learned in an evening. It will take months, perhaps years."

52

"All right," Danny said. "Provided that I'm reasonably sure the investment is worth the risk. What's the essential principle?"

The woman's coarse face became transfigured by an expression Danny could describe only as sappy.

"Love," she said.

At the same moment, the word appeared, wavering, inside the crystal globe, projected in what looked to be Old English or Wedding Text type. A faint squeak accompanied it, like the sound of a sewing-machine treadle in need of oil.

"Oh," Danny said. "Well, that gives me a fine start. I've just had a short refresher course in that, and it didn't seem to take months, either. What's the method?"

"You must return here twice a week. We shall begin by seeking the advice of Those Who Have Gone Before. Eventually we shall practice apports, and if we are fortunate we shall be allowed to study the manipulation of ectoplasm. If all goes well, we will at last achieve full contact."

"I can make faster progress than that by myself, I'm afraid," Danny said. "Thanks for listening, but I'll have to stick to my own methods, after all. Damned if I wanted to."

The woman's eyes abruptly went into deep-freeze.

"Very well," she rumbled. "That will be five dollars, young man."

Danny looked away from the bestial reflection of the woman's face on the surface of the smoky globe, a foretaste of the pig-god of passion who ruled the myths she spoke for, and scanned the room. The girl was gone, still.

53

He dug in his wallet, and was vaguely surprised to find that he still had a five-dollar bill. After a brief double-take, he put it back again and took out two singles.

"For services rendered," he said, more sardonically than he had intended.

Mme. Zaza glared and her lips worked for an instant. Then she took the proffered money, the muscles standing out at the angle of her jaw. It was evident Danny was anything but her usual kind of customer. She turned her back on him and disappeared behind the scarlet hangings.

The girl was in the bare front room as Danny went out, sitting on the edge of the table and swinging idly one intensely feminine leg, which issued from the Puritanical skirt like the heresy which ends an era.

She raised one eyebrow at him. "Get your money's worth?" she said. The words came out in abrupt jerks, as if she had not intended to speak and was angry to find herself speaking all the same.

Danny smiled tentatively. "I got what I deserved, anyhow," he said.

She shrugged. "You looked moderately sensible. Not the usual sucker. I wondered whether you'd be taken in by all that guff."

Danny was surprised into laughing. The girl's expression became angrier.

"That's a funny way for a medium's apprentice to talk."

"I'm no apprentice. I'm just a prop girl. I blow cigarette smoke into the glass egg, and make the trumpet talk, and all that. My aunt supplies the patter." She looked at him directly while she spoke, but her stare was unreadable;
54

Danny could not tell whether it was his wallet, his skull, or his clothing that she was looking through.

"You didn't answer me," she said. "What's brought you here? Or—are you from the cops?"

"No, I'm not. What I told your aunt was the literal truth. Somehow I've developed a couple of abnormal talents that I don't understand, and they've already gotten me into a jam—two jams, really, and a third one probably coming up. Under the circumstances, I'm willing to pick up information anywhere I can find it."

"You won't get it from a medium," the girl said. "You must be having bad dreams."

"No, I'm not," Danny insisted, becoming a little irritated. He wondered if the girl, too, were going to tell him to visit a psychoanalyst. Her unwavering regard made him extremely uncomfortable, and the idly swinging leg, its image falling upon the fovea of his eye with metronomic, almost intromittent rhythm, was ticking his ability to conduct a reasonable conversation (or any conversation) away into a kind of deep hypnosis. A direct look at the leg would have put it back into the universe in its proper proportion, placed it on his retina in relation to the rest of the world, but Danny could not bring himself to move his eyes from the girl's face while she was watching him with that puzzling, unspecified intensity.

"How do you know?"

"Because for the most part, well, plenty has happened to me in broad daylight, that's all."

"Bad dreams can last for weeks. They can last all your life. Ask any steady customer at Bellevue."

"I know that. But I've got a fair collection of what

55

seems to be good evidence, objective evidence. And I expect to have positive proof of one part of it by Friday."

"Remember what they say about the paving stones in Hell," the girl said. "You've had a gush of balderdash to the head, that's all. Otherwise you wouldn't be here. You could have found everything you needed to know about mediums in the public library; everybody knows about Houdini's book."

Underneath the smoking, sullen scorn in her voice, there was a faint hint of something else—was it disappointment? Danny couldn't tell. He said carefully, "I don't think it's balderdash, I didn't know Houdini had written anything about mediums, and in any event nobody has been playing tricks on me. You and your aunt tried; it didn't take."

There was again the slightest change in the girl's expression, but again Danny could not read it. He concluded: "I may quite possibly be crazy. As a matter of fact, that's the assumption I'm working on, tentatively. But I'm not a fool."

"Then why don't you stop acting like one?" she said, getting up.

The motion was like that of a stalking cat. Danny's battered good temper suddenly collapsed before it. Without any warning, a blinding stab of pain shot through his head. In the foreground of his skull he became vividly, maddeningly conscious of a thousand billion tiny things, whirling and whirling in a vast shimmer of movement. Rainbows wheeled before him with the rapidity and glare of lightning.

For an instant he was blind. He took a heavy step backward. The pain increased; the whirling became faster.

56

The girl loomed, a black-on-black composition of matched curves; then, behind her, a straight line which could only be the table-top, cutting through her thighs. The straight line became solid, as if the girl were melting—

The table canted and shot skyward. It struck the ceiling a heavy blow. Plaster showered on his shoulders and head.

Now he could see again, but the whirling pain continued. The table, still pressed against the ceiling, slid sidewise, like a monstrous spider. A second later, one of the chairs teetered hesitantly on one leg and then leaped after it.

The girl screamed and pressed back against the wall, dwindling out of his attention except as a disturbing mass somewhere in the vicinity. Danny stood, frozen all the way in to his diaphragm, the whirling of the thousand billion tiny things wrapping his maddened brain in agony.

Mme. Zaza ripped the rug aside. "What the hell? Hey you, what goes on here?"

There was a flash of colorless fire, and it was all gone. The chair and table fell straight down. The table hit near a corner, and one leg splintered and snapped in the middle.

Released, Danny staggered to right himself.

"You get out of here!" Mme. Zaza said, with concentrated viciousness. "Get out before I call the cops. I'm a decent woman and I've got a license. I won't have slobs wrecking my place. Out, God damn you, get out—"

Evidently the hairy woman had seen nothing except something normal, or, at the least, explicable, though she had been looking directly and with blank fury at the furniture bumping along the ceiling. Danny managed

57

an ironical bow; it would hardly have lit the *Tilt* light on a pinball machine, but it gave him some satisfaction.

"Only a small demonstration," he murmured, slurring his words uncontrollably. He walked carefully to the door and went out.

The girl watched him go, one hand thrown across her mouth, her eyes wide. In another girl, that expression would have meant fright. What it meant on this girl's face he could not tell, and he was anxious not to find out. He grinned at her through the smeared window, flagged a cab, and watched her shrink out of his ken until he could no longer see the shop at all.

Then she was gone, around a corner. Danny slumped upon the cushions of the cab, nothing left in him but the residues of his loss, and the consciousness of a new wild talent.

If there were any wilder ones, it would be nice never to have to know a thing about them.

He was hardly inside his own apartment when the telephone burst into a nerve-shattering outcry. Swearing, Danny crossed the room and snatched up the handset.

"*Hall*-o," he snapped.

"Hello, Danny, where the hell have you been? Are you okay?"

"Who wants to—oh, it's you, Sean. Yeah, I'm all right, I guess. I've been downtown all afternoon."

"Doing what?"

"Poking around the stock market."

"You *were?*" Sean sounded incredulous; he seemed to be able to detect the effluvium of half-truth, however faint. Yet what right did he have, after all, to a full explanation? Danny began to feel resentful again.

"You had me scared to death," Sean was saying. "I thought maybe you had passed out on the subway or something—I was nearly ready to set the cops to looking for you, phoning hospitals, and all that. If I ever marry I'll swear a solemn oath against fatherhood, I'd go nuts keeping track of the sprats. Danny, why don't you stay home a day or so and get some rest? You need it."

Danny was suspended halfway between laughter and an explosion of the purest, anhydrous vitriol. "Why do I need it?" he said carefully.

"Well, the obvious reason. You've been working for Delta for God knows how long; Delta allows its editors only a week of vacation at a time; you had your first week five months ago. Why don't you take the other? God knows you earned it, even if Delta didn't pay you for it."

"Look, Sean," Danny said. "You don't have to take the whole world on your shoulders on my account. I appreciate it in a way, but it crowds me a bit, too. Your children don't have to be monitored up and down every curbstone."

"Ah, there's a Parthian shot. But what am I to think, Danny? You took me in on your troubles, so I need to know."

"I guess you do . . . Well, I've got something funny by the tail, that's all. I don't mean to let go of it. But I'm satisfied that my sanity's okay, and my health, too. That's all."

"Well, all right," Sean said dubiously. "Let me know if you need any help from me."

"Sure. You can start right now. Do you remember the

59

name of the writer who collected all that dope about wild talents? The press associations used to mention him about twice a week all during the silly season."

Sean snorted. "The silly season! Are you out to make it a national celebration? But I know the man you mean: his name was Fort, Charles Fort. There's a cult of Forteans here in town. Do you want to talk to them?"

"I might," Danny said. "I'm not any less improbable in my own mind now than a flying saucer. Oh, and another thing—do you happen to know if there's a branch of the Psychic Research Society here?"

"I'm sure there is; they must be in the phone book. Are you making a collection of fellow-fruitcakes, Danny? If so, you might as well go out to the University too, and throw dice with the parapsychology boys there."

"Good—I'll do that," Danny said. "That's fine, Sean. Any other suggestions?"

"You've heard my other one," Sean said evenly. He sounded, Danny thought, a little disgusted, though he could not be quite sure.

"See an analyst, eh?"

"That's it."

There was an awkward silence.

Danny said: "Okay, Sean. I'll think about it. Don't worry, and thanks a lot. I'll be seeing you, when I can."

"So long," Sean said.

For a moment after he hung up, Danny sat in his chair, frowning at nothing. Sean puzzled him: big-hearted, cheerful always, absurdly generous, quick to take offence at injustices which affected him personally hardly or not at all—yet somehow unstable, incalculable, evasive as mercury. His buoyant voice over the telephone, inexplicably concerned yet also as serene and confident as the late-summer snoring of a cicada, was a sound which Danny found harder to understand than any of his own wrestling-matches with the irrational. He could relate it to nothing, least of all to the easy reasons whose advocate Sean seemed to be.

But, at least, Sean had seemed to have been a bit offended at Danny's stubborn failure to accept the explanation of simple psychosis. And he had offered help, and had provided something vaguely like understanding; and obviously he would like to be allowed in on Danny's next moves. He'd quit his own job in Danny's behalf; he was, as he had pleaded, entitled to know.

Danny considered calling him back and letting him in on the stock market deal. But then he thought better of it. Sean had not evinced any interest in it. He had hardly been able to believe it. Too, Sean had very little money of his own—when he had first come to Delta he had been living in a single cold-water room on Orchard Street ("Two blocks away," he had said, "from New York's main clearing-house for vest-pocket pornography") with a theatrical and handsome Negro pacifist who spent most of his time in futile tours of India and remoter places at the expense of some desperate, multi-denominational, astonishingly Christian group, leaving the flat unoccupied except for Sean and the tea he poured on his cornflakes because he could not keep milk—and there would be no point in tormenting him with an opportunity he could not take, even were he inclined to credit it.

Danny took out his wallet and looked through it. He

61

discovered that the three presumptive one-dollar bills which he had given the cabby had included instead the one remaining fiver he had had. He had left two dollars, plus whatever change he could find in his few intact pockets. Small wonder that the hackey had been so polite, there at the very end of the long ride.

It was almost dark. Danny closed the cardboard Venetian blinds and put on the desk lamp. At the desk, after a search for a pen, he wrote a letter to himself, outlining in painful detail a number of things that hadn't happened yet, and specifying when they would happen. This he addressed to himself.

For all he knew so far, the letter might be waste motion. Though he could never be sure, he thought he needed no proof for himself. But he might need help—and the postmark on that letter might serve him well later as evidence.

Or it might not. Nevertheless, he sealed the letter with great care, and stamped it, and put it on the straight chair by the door, where he'd be sure to see it when he went out tomorrow.

Then he had nothing to do but undress, which turned out to be a hard task in itself. He saw no sleep in sight. It was queer, for instance, about the ponies. Surely predicting the outcome of a horse-race was essentially simpler than foreknowing what a complicated set of factors like the stock market was going to do. Still, he'd hit the horses twice. That might have been just chance, and then again—

For the trick of throwing the medium's furniture around, he refused to attempt any explanation. Even thinking about it made reminiscent pain begin to burn beneath his forehead.

He gulped down an aspirin, but without much hope. He was already hiccupping with nervousness, and his hands were shaking.

With dancing fingers he set the alarm clock for the hour when he would have to have awakened in order to get to the lost job. The backs of his legs ached profoundly. He was tired: tired. He was able to wonder whether or not he had overlooked a bet, but he was far too gone to understand the question once he had asked it of the dead, celibate air. He sank onto the cot, his second sock still not quite off, with a gasp of exhaustion; and for a long while, sweating, he imagined himself asleep.

Then . . . dimly . . . in the hot, still air, soundless voices murmured together:

"The tension gathers. It is real now."

"Danger. I estann a real danger."

"Yes, but we are prepared. Let us wait."

"Yes, wait."

Danny, still imagining himself asleep, stirred. Sweat poured off his sides onto the clammy sheets. The sinister convocation proceeded, deep in the earth.

"The walker draws near, my brother; very near."

"Let him beware then."

"But the danger—"

"—Caveat inventor. That is the rule. Let the finder beware."

The voices took up their discussion of things beyond comprehension, beyond all eavesdropping.

An icy dew dwindled over Danny's forehead. Somewhere in the black night there was a bubbling pain, and a spinning of a thousand billion tiny things. He felt light and giddy. He felt himself turning over, slowly.

In the dream, he seemed to open his eyes and look downward, without surprise, at a deserted, streetlamp-lit road, ten stories down.

The tingling, the pain, the whirling increased, like an old story impossible to forget. A man went by down below, his legs alternating absurdly under his shoulders. Danny floated.

After a while, he felt a vague alarm that he should even be dreaming such a thing. He willed himself to move.

Gently, he began to drift. The street revolved solemnly out of his view; now he saw stars, and the sheer diminishing side of the building, ending in the constellation of Auriga, a winter trapehedron up in summer only because he was himself floating late and damned in nothing and on nothing in the wet summer air.

Terrified, he drove himself. Heels first, he went back into his room, floating, bobbing a little, on his back. The gulf beneath him faded. The window swallowed him.

Then he was on his bed again, on his back, swimming in sweat. The dream was over.

If it had been a dream.

chapter six

~~~~~~

EDUCATION OF AN ACOLYTE

Danny stood up as Dr. Todd came out of his office. The parapsychologist was a small, bald, and totally engaging man, full of bounce, quite unlike any professor Danny had ever seen before—and certainly most unlike the man with a monomania that Sean had foreshadowed. Todd had been more than helpful, though he would have been justified in refusing Danny's demand to be tested ahead of the laboratory's regular schedule.

"Well, Mr. Caiden," the parapsychologist said, "I really don't know what made you think you were especially gifted parapsychologically. We've just codified most of the results, and I'm safe in saying that your psi quotient —that's our index of an individual's parapsychological powers—seems quite thoroughly moronic." He sat down and polished his glasses solemnly.

Danny frowned. "No indication at all?"

"Nothing indicative. Of course, we can't say definitely until we've tested you over a period of several months— preferably over several years, which is probably impossible, since you're not a student at the University, as most of our regular test subjects are. But the sampling tests show no better than average chance results on the cards and the dice both."

"Oh," Danny said, grinning. "Then I can't really be a moron, or my score would have been *below* the chance average."

"Don't you believe it," said Todd. "In this kind of work, a score consistently below average is just as inexplicable by the laws of chance as is a score consistently above it. We have trunksful of data indicating strong negative effects on chance, exercised by people with strong psi quotients who were nervous, upset, anxious about their showings, and so on. Calm such people down and run them again under good conditions, and their scores go up like rockets."

"I begin to see. Considering my emotional state, my involvement, and such factors, I should have shown a negative effect, then."

"Well, that's what I would have expected, had you shown any abilities along our line," the parapsychologist said cheerfully. "But you haven't so far, my boy. That is, you're no good at the cards or the dice. Don't forget that our experimental techniques explore only the most rudimentary kind of exercise of the psi faculties. You may be in the position of a master chef being asked to make a shapely mud pie. You might be able to do it, but then again—"

"That's letting me down easy," Danny said. "But you could be right at that. Is there any more?"

"Oh, certainly. This is just a preamble. We have other

results, too. I only wanted to prepare you for the fact that we can't make head or tail of them, and to let you know that our usual tests drew blanks. Take your electro-encephalograms, for instance. Do you know how the machine works?"

"Yes, I think so, Dr. Todd. The brain is supposed to generate a small amount of electricity as it operates, and the encephalograph sort of picks up the broadcast and writes it out in the form of a curve."

"Very good," Todd said, looking pleased and a little surprised. "Well, your alpha wave pattern—the normal wave output of your brain while at rest—is totally out of the ordinary. It follows the general curve that the usual human being's alpha pattern does; but there is a regular series of secondary modulations that are quite new to me."

"But you don't know what it means?"

"In the light of what you've told me about yourself, I can at least make a guess," Todd said cautiously. "Remember that the alpha pattern represents the activity of the brain *at rest*. A sort of general repair and maintenance function. Conscious intellection is reflected in the gamma wave, which we don't fuss with simply because we've never found a subject whose psi abilities were enough under his control to show up as gamma wave activity.

"Tentatively, we can say that at least one other part of your brain which nobody else uses—even when thinking—is in continuous operation for you. It's not an activity of your cerebral cortex, your 'gray matter.' It's some submerged, every-minute-of-the-day activity of which you're not conscious, any more than you're conscious of the death and renewal of worn-out cells. To carry the guess still further, we'll say that this new function may be located in the four-fifths of your brain for which no function is known right now; certainly it doesn't conform to any of the sensory wave responses that we know. We may be able to confirm that when the X-rays come through; I certainly hope so. We do have a few crude methods for recognizing ESP subcortical activity, though we seldom find it."

"ESP?"

"Extra sensory perception. Dr. Rhine gave the psi faculties that general name after it turned out that they don't function anything like the other two dozen or so known senses."

"Two dozen—whoa, Dr. Todd. I thought there were only five, but if there are two dozen I'll take your word for it without any explanation. I'd like to stick to my own troubles. They confuse me enough as it is." He rubbed his head ruefully. "One thing I know from personal experience: ESP hurts when it's working, I'll guarantee that."

"Naturally. You're opening up new synapses, new impulse-channels from nerve-cell to cell. Many of them have never been used before, and, for all we know, they may still be in a highly primitive state. One of the things we're trying to find out is whether ESP is something man had once and gradually lost, or whether it's something brand new that he's developing. In either case, though, it should get easier each time you use the new channels, just like establishing a habit or a training pattern.

"But that's not what we want to get at, basically.

68

Those individual synapses are just building-blocks for two very general brain-functions. ESP is the most widely known one, but PK, psychokinesis, is just as important. ESP helps you detect things—objects, events, thoughts. PK enables you to act on them—as, for instance, when our more gifted people influence the way dice fall. All these side-effects, such as precognition and telepathy, are simply different manifestations of these two basic functions, just as colors are just different manifestations of light."

"Or light and radio of the electromagnetic spectrum as a whole?"

"Bravo," said Todd, looking surprised again. "I must say, I wish one year of college physics 'took' as well with most college students as it seems to have done with you."

He broke off as an assistant entered the room quietly, carrying with him a small stack of films. "Ah," Todd said, "Let's take a look."

Danny took a look, over Todd's shoulder. "Those don't look like any X-rays I ever saw before," he said.

Todd chuckled. "They aren't," he said. "But we call them X-rays for convenience, since this process hasn't got a standard name of its own yet. Actually it's a development of tracer chemistry, an outgrowth of the development of the fission bomb. We've discovered that the element ekacesium has an affinity for the subcortical Golgi bodies, just as iodine has an affinity for the cells of the thyroid gland. So we give you a little artificially-radio-active ekacesium—you remember the shot we gave you—and after a while we put some X-ray plates against your head and waited to see what would happen. The second shot, which shows up on these three plates on the bottom

69

of the stack, contained radio-silver; that's strictly cortical, homing on your gray matter. We felt we couldn't afford to miss any bets."

He held the plates up to the viewer, one by one. Danny watched anxiously.

"There's some concentration here," Todd muttered. "More than I've ever seen before, that's certain already. Hard to tell how it's shaping up. But we'll get it. Suppose you come back tomorrow, Danny. I've got a little book-work to do; you've confronted me with a situation I didn't expect even my grandchildren would have to cope with. Then we'll make a fresh attack."

Danny could not repress his disappointment. "Do you think there's any hope?" he said.

"Hope?" the parapsychologist exploded. "Great jumping grasshoppers, man, you bring me the first chance we've ever had to observe this What-Is-It we call the psi faculties directly, and you ask me if there's any hope! Skin out of here before I crown you and spoil the specimen."

Danny left, feeling a little better, his head still full of the squares, stars, crosses, wavy lines and circles on Dr. Todd's test cards. The results were exciting, yet discouragingly inconclusive; to Danny, who needed to know *now*, the inexorable working-out of scientific method seemed likely to be fatally lengthy.

Well, that was to have been expected. It was hard to imagine any normal, everyday agency, even one as un-orthodox as the parapsychology labs, coming to grips with the outlandish Unknowns that were invading Danny's head. He was lucky that Dr. Todd had gotten even as far as he had. The man's confidence, at least, was infectious enough to make Danny feel a little less despairing.

The Forteans were even less helpful, though friendly. The local branch of the Fortean Society had only a post office box address. When he finally found them, it was by way of *Who's Who*. Their local leader turned out to be Cartier Taylor, a popular author, a man who had written so many colorful and occasionally acute thrillers that even Danny had heard of him. Indeed, the Fortean group seemed to be crawling with writers of various calibres, most of whom were more impressed by their Master's brilliant writing style than with his disordered metaphysical theories.

Taylor, a slickly handsome man past middle age in the process of going to seed, but with a gift for brilliantly bitter chatter which dazzled Danny into complete inarticulateness, was more than willing to load Danny up with half a hundred reports of wild talents of every conceivable kind. He had bins of them, collected by assiduous Forteans all over the world, and filed under such titles as "Pyrotics," "Poltergeists," "Rains of Frogs," and "Oil-Prones." But nothing that he had to offer in the way of theories to account for such reports seemed better than idiotic. Indeed, he seemed to have a special bias toward the idiotic, and to be out to trap Danny into every possible concession that "orthodox" theories of the state of the universe were nonsense.

He viewed scientists-in-the-mass as a kind of priesthood, and scientific method as a new form of mumbo-jumbo. This twist made him partial to astrology, hollow-earth notions, Lemuria, pyramidology, phrenology, Vedanta,

71

black magic, Koresanity, Theosophy, Rosicrucianism, crystalline atoms, lunar farming, Atlantis, and a long list of similar asininities—the more asinine the better. At bottom, however, every one of these beliefs (if Taylor believed in any of them; Danny could not tell whether he subscribed to any given doctrine because he liked it or only because he liked to be in revolt against anything more generally accepted) turned out to rest upon some form of personal-devil theory: Roosevelt had sold the world down the river, the world press was out to suppress reports of unorthodox happenings, astronomers conspired to wangle money for useless instruments, physicists were secretly planning to promote the purchase of cyclotrons by high schools, the Catholic Church was about to shut down independent thinking throughout the United States, doctors were promoting useless or dangerous drugs because they were expensive—all with the glossiest of plausible surfaces, all as mad as the maddest asylum-shuttered obsession of direct persecution. Danny was not at all surprised that Taylor was determinedly and brilliantly trying to sell him Dianetics as Danny backed out of the door of the writer's apartment.

Yet Fort himself assuredly made exciting reading, as Danny found directly afterward at the public library. He could see why writers loved the man. He wrote in a continuous and highly poetic display of verbal fireworks, superbly controlled, intricately balanced, witty and evocative at once. His attitude toward his world seemed to be a sort of cosmic flatulence, about midway between the irony of Heine epigrams which Danny remembered well and Ritz Brothers slapstick which he would be happy to forget.

72

But, like Taylor, his explanations for the things he had observed, collected at second hand, or simply collated were deliberately outrageous. Every now and then Danny found in one or another of Fort's four books a glimmering trail toward something useful—and every time Fort took the developing insight and stood it on its head, or worse, distorted it into complete childishness.

A scientist with a sense of humor and more than usual patience with sloppy thinking might have made something of Fort's *Wild Talents*, the one book of the four which bore centrally upon Danny's troubles. But for Danny, who had no scientific training and a desperate need to know *now* what it was all about, there was nothing to be found but the assurance that a lot of other people had been in his fix, or something rather like it.

Other books claimed his attention, though he had no systematic way of knowing what to look for or how to look for it. It was easy enough to find the books by Dr. Rhine, and the medium's niece had mentioned a book by Houdini, which turned out to be called *A Magician Among Spirits*—not, Danny thought, a very promising title. After that it became more difficult. Littleton's *Our Superconscious Mind* turned up only after a hard search from one cross-reference to another, and Tyrrell's *Science and Psychical Phenomena* he would have missed entirely had he not remembered seeing the card while searching out the Houdini book.

After that he had to stab at random, painfully conscious of the possibly crucial works which he must be missing. He came to Dunne's *An Experiment with Time* only by a hairline coincidence: he had seen a discussion of Dunne

73

in Priestly's popular *Midnight on the Desert*, and the writer's name had leapt out at him while he was looking for "dowsing" among the cards.

The last book he took out was by Ouspenskii—the *Tertium Organum*. He had come to this, too, by a roundabout and utterly unscientific way. A book review of T. S. Eliot's *Four Quartets* had mentioned the same writer's *A New Model of the Universe*, and curiosity had led him to buy it, though he had up to now been unable to read it; the first book he had never heard of, but finding it in the cards had been enough for him. Before leaving the library, he also considered de Camp's *Adventures in the Occult*, but a brief page-through convinced him that this was essentially debunkery—sane and sound enough, without question, but the opposite side of the Fortean coin, out to knock down all unorthodoxies as a matter of course; hence, not likely to be of much help to a man in the toils of the apparently indefensible.

And that left him only the Psychic Research Society.

Danny had had no idea of what he had expected to find there: a group of mediums, perhaps, struggling to make their trade respectable—a quasi-religious organization hoping to prove survival after death—something more dubious and useless, in any event, than anything his previous searches had turned up.

He was totally unprepared to meet Sir Lewis Carter.

He recognized the internationally famous astronomer and science popularizer at once. His mismatched trousers and jacket, his calabash pipe with the meerschaum top, were almost as familiar as trademarks. The scientist was standing in the foyer of the old brownstone which housed the PRS, but he turned as Danny swung open the heavy door, and the light from outside fell full on him.

Danny was too surprised to speak for a moment. Then he said: "Don't tell me you're the boss of this outfit, sir?"

Sir Lewis inclined his iron-gray head. "More or less, young fella. What's your problem? But come in to the office; no need to share our conversation with the umbrella-jug."

Inside, Danny gave him a quick sketch, leaving out the flatly incredible parts. It was substantially the same story he had told Sean. Sir Lewis made no comment until he was through. Then he said:

"Have you seen anybody else about this?"

"Just about everybody," Danny said. "Even the Forteans and the ESP people at the University."

Sir Lewis dismissed Dr. Rhine's disciples with a wave of his pipestem. "You got nothing out of that crowd, I'll warrant. They can't seem to realize that you can't handle things as delicate as psychic manifestations as if they were performing dogs. These phenomena have their own special laws, and they're pretty stubborn about failing to show up except under special conditions."

Danny felt uncomfortable. Even Fort had seen through that old argument. Fresh from his research, he remembered Fort's damning observation that authentic teleportations and other para-normal events always occur openly. *These data would make trouble for spiritualistic mediums and their requirements for special, or closed, conditions . . . Nobody in this house sat in a cabinet . . . "For instance," said nobody, "how could you develop a photograph, except in the special conditions of darkness, or*

75

semi-darkness?" And then there had been a sardonic description of a chemist actually forced to work under similar conditions, sitting in the dark holding hands with laymen and asking whether or not there was anybody present who had an affinity for a chemical named Hydrogen.

And Fort had been a cipher as a scientist; what was Sir Lewis doing advancing this old chestnut? Danny decided not to ask. It was difficult not to be awed by so much fame in the flesh. Instead he said: "That sounds reasonable. What I want to know mainly is how to control these—well, these powers. The way they keep popping up is damned uncomfortable. They've lost me my job, and I suspect I'll be in worse trouble before very long."

And that, he added mentally, ought to win this year's medal for understatement.

"I quite sympathize," Sir Lewis said gravely. "What I suggest is that you stay with us here for observation, until we can get a firm grip on the nature of the powers you're coming into. We can make you quite comfortable, and we'll then have plenty of opportunity to study these manifestations as they occur. We have funds for that purpose, so you needn't worry about a job for the time being; and you'll be—so to speak—off the street, and thus out of any serious danger."

"That's generous of you," Danny said. "But unfortunately I have so many things to keep track of that I can't risk it right now. I wasn't exaggerating when I said I was in a mess. Would later be all right?"

"Quite all right; suit yourself," Sir Lewis said. "Let me see, I have your address. I'll send you some literature; you may find something useful there."

76

"Thanks," Danny said.

"Thank you, Mr. Caiden. Please call me if I can help you in any way. I think you will find your situation becoming very difficult before long."

"I believe you," Danny said stolidly.

chapter seven

~~~~~~

CALLS AND ANSWERS

On the subway back to his apartment, Danny scanned a late paper. He turned to the financial section first, only to find that the International Wheat headline there was over a "jump"—a continuation from another page, which turned out to be the front page of the paper. Wheat had gotten its indictment, and the market had already slid three points. Dow-Jones experts were beginning to worry learnedly about a "penetration"—a break through the previous low point which usually indicated a general slump and a bearish market; perhaps even, if it went much farther, a real crash.

Proof!

Danny was glad that he'd mailed that letter. Curiously, he had encountered far less scepticism during his researches than he had expected—less than he liked, now that he came to think of it. He would not need the letter to get an audience with others, as he had thought he would. But it did wonders for his own torment of self-inquisition.

It was far too late in the day for him to pick up his earnings on the venture, but they'd still be available Monday, and would be more than handy to have. He should be able to last for many weeks on them. But why hadn't the sense of prediction worked just as well at the races? Couldn't this damnable sense for the future be brought under control? No one freak success, no matter how happy, could solve that basic and fatal problem.

He had had a triumph, but a shadowed one.

There was a small knot of people, mostly women, gathered in the lobby of the apartment building when Danny arrived. One of them, a portly well-dressed man Danny recognized in a double-take as his landlord, detached himself from the group as soon as Danny came through the outer door. The women drew back, and whispered hoarsely.

"Mr. Caiden, might I speak to you for a moment, privately?"

"Certainly," Danny said. They went through the inner door, leaving the women humming like telephone dial-tones in the lobby.

"I'm afraid I'm going to have to ask you to vacate these premises," the landlord said, the moment they were safely in the stairwell. "I regard myself as a broadminded man, Mr. Caiden, but most of my tenants are middle class and rather censorious, and do not consider the maintenance of young women in bachelor apartments as an asset to the general community."

It took Danny a moment to get the pompous sentence unwound; he had not been paying very close attention. "Young women?" he echoed feebly.

"Perhaps I should have spoken in the singular; but I

79

anticipate myself. I was called here by Mrs. Tafuri, of Eight-A, anent a disturbance centering about your apartment," the landlord intoned. "As I have the story, and after eliminating points of conflict between the various versions supplied by other tenants, Mrs. Tafuri observed a young lady leaving a taxicab in front of this building, and then entering it.

"Mrs. Emerson of Six-F reports having heard your doorbell ring, after which—some minutes after—the young lady was heard to be mounting the stairs and admitting herself to your apartment with a passkey." He took a deep breath and belly-whopped into another sentence.

"Later on, the superintendent, a man of tested and impeccable veracity, I might say, who had been called out by telephone to repair a plumbing leak—a *non-existent* leak, I might add—reported a passkey missing, this being a passkey from the boardhook bearing the number of your apartment; and, at the same time, Mrs. Schoenbrun, who lives in the apartment beneath you, heard footsteps crossing her ceiling, and since she is a nearly deaf old lady with an interest in spirits reported the matter to the real estate office under the impression that she was being haunted, an impression which we are inclined to deplore; the landlord inquired in the meantime about the passkey and was informed by Mrs. Flores of Two-B that—"

Danny had long ago heard enough. He bounded up the stairs, leaving the landlord floundering in a welter of dependent clauses. Unaccountably, his hand trembled under his own doorknob, making the front tooth of his key chatter against the violated lock.

The girl was there, all right; she watched him enter with

80

that same smoldering surliness, without moving an inch from where she sat. Danny slammed the door and locked and bolted it. A moment later, the portly, pompous ass outside was pounding on the thin panelling.

"Twenty-four hours!" he shouted, syntax forgotten in sheer rage at being first abandoned and then shut out. "An eviction notice! Respectable house! Won't have it! Law and order! Do you hear?"

"Yah," Danny said. "I'll leave. Beat it. You're waking up my spiders."

The closed door emitted a choked inspiration.

Danny turned his back on it and glared at the girl. She was sitting in his favorite armchair, smoking one of the emperor-sized cigarettes he favored when he was alone. The glass tube it had come in lay beside her on the telephone table. She eyed Danny with cool amusement.

"What are you doing here?" he growled.

"Waiting for you," she said. "And in case you're wondering how I knew where you lived, I heard you give your address to the cabby when you left my aunt's place."

"You didn't look like you had presence of mind enough left to overhear an air raid siren."

"I specialize in hearing what I need to hear, and in getting what I need to get. In the first case, your address; in the second, your secrets. By the way, my name's Marla."

"I'm Danny Caiden," he said automatically. Then: "The hell you say! I'll keep my secrets to myself, thanks. What do you actually want of me, anyhow? You've lost me my apartment, and I'm in enough trouble already."

"With your talents," she said with dangerous sweetness,

F

"I'm sure you could conjure up another one out of nothing. And I'm going to be on the spot to see it done, too."

"Like hell you are. You're going to get out of here pronto, or I'll pitch you out, right on that derrière you're pointing at me."

"No, you won't," Marla said. "I'll scream. You'll go to jail. That wouldn't be nice."

He glared at her. "What is this—a shakedown? I haven't any money, and right now I don't give two cents for a rape charge. You couldn't make it stick, and you've already done me all the damage possible among my neighbors."

"I don't want your money. What you've got is worth more to me than money. And I don't want your personal secrets, either—just your professional ones. Don't pull an act on Marla, Danny; she's a bright girl. You know just as well as I do what a professional magician means by a 'secret'—you're a professional, and one of the best. Judging by the drasticness of your effects, I'd say you were a student of Thurston's, though you look a mite young for that."

"You gabble. I saw Thurston once when I was seven years old. He stuffed a pack of cards in my mouth and cut the corners of it, my mouth I mean, in about nineteen places. I was one of a flock of about thirty kids on stage. Now *what do you want?*"

"I want to know how that trick of yours was pulled—the way you threw the table and chair around. You did it without any previous preparation, and in a place you'd never seen before, as far as I know. No secret in the catalogues matches it. It'll mow the suckers down in droves. What else can you do?"

"If I stick my tongue out a certain way," Danny said

sardonically, "I can make a noise like a turtle-dove." He was about to demonstrate when it struck him that to do the trick he had not only to stick his tongue out but also to roll it lengthwise like a cigar-leaf. Though he had done it cheerfully before for more girls than he could reckon at the moment, he decided abruptly that he was not going to do it under the level regard of this one. "As for pitching your furniture around, I'm beating my brains out trying to find out for myself how I do it. It's as big a secret to me as it is to you. When I do find out, I'll keep in practise by zipping your zipper up and down and tying granny knots in your shoelaces. Now will you go?"

"Nope. I'm sticking until I find out how it's done. You're a very good liar, Danny, but I've seen Dunninger—and I don't believe in spirits."

Danny threw himself into the rocking chair, which he hated, and then threw himself out again hastily; the expanse of nylon which turned out to be visible from the rocker would have made it impossible to think at all. He went over to the washstand and washed his hands.

"What about your aunt?" he said in desperation.

"That old harridan?" Marla laughed scornfully. There was a whisper behind his back, as if she were moving in the armchair. "She'll never get any farther than she's gotten now. She just uses the same old routines and won't learn anything. Marla's different. She's out for smart suckers— suckers who can't be fooled by tricks that bored Houdini to death. I know a brand new line when I see one, and I don't mean to let go of it."

The whisper came again. She added: "Even if I have to marry it."

83

"I see," Danny said, scrubbing. "I was wondering when you'd get to that. I don't like to spoil the evening, Marla, but you'll have to get it through your head that I haven't a damned thing to sell, not even at that price."

For some reason, his chest hurt him; he had to pause a moment. "Otherwise you'd probably have yourself a deal, if that's any consolation."

"*No, I wouldn't,*" the girl's voice said, each word flatly and evenly spaced. "I didn't come here to sleep with you. If I had, I would have said so. If I decide later that I want to, I will, and if you offer me a secret or the Taj Mahal or twenty-five cents afterwards I'll split you up like a moldy tangerine. I was talking about marrying you before you changed the subject."

"You don't sleep with your husbands, of course. You just eat them."

"You're as vile as any other American. I sleep where I choose until I have a contract. If I have to sign a contract with you I'll do it. You'll have to sign too. God help you if you don't observe it—and in the meantime, keep your bed. I'll bet you haven't changed it in weeks."

Danny was about to say that he had changed it only five days ago when somebody knocked sharply. The soap skidded out of Danny's now puckered and spotless fingers.

"Go 'way," Danny grated. "I told you I'd leave. Blow."

There was a short, puzzled silence. Then the knock came again. Evidently it wasn't the landlord this time. Cautiously Danny turned the lock, shot back the bolt, and peered out through an opening hardly wider than a hairpin.

The knocker wore a gray business suit and a gray fedora,

and looked a little like an inefficient CPA. He said, "Mr. Caiden?"

"That's me."

"FBI," the knocker said, flopping his wallet open under Danny's nose. The card in the wallet said the same thing. Silently, Danny stepped back to let him in.

"Thank you. I'd like to talk to you. I think you're in trouble, Mr. Caiden."

"I'll save a five-column streamer on the front page for that story. What's the matter now? Don't tell me the landlord's decided to invoke the Mann Act!"

Marla's expression became blisteringly cold. She looked pointedly out the window at the developing night.

"No, Mr. Caiden, we're not interested in your home life. I'm here on behalf of the Securities Exchange Commission, as well as the FBI. I expect you were too young to have noticed the '29 crash, but we're anxious to see that it doesn't happen again. Smart operators who are out to make it happen again—or who operate as if they don't care if it does—get our deep-freeze treatment, but quick."

"What puts me in that category?" Danny asked carefully.

"What you pulled today was suggestive, to say the least," the FBI man said. He sat down calmly in the rocking chair and crossed his legs. He didn't bother to take off his hat; it looked as if it had grown there. He took a good look at Marla's knees before proceeding, as if he already owned everything he might encounter anywhere in the world.

"Your ex-employers name you as the man who broke the Attorney General's secret indictment of International

85

Wheat, not only before the release date, but before the release had even been mimeo'ed. Today we find you the only investor on the market who caught IW short when the break following the indictment came through, except for a few laymen who would follow any tip including out-and-out astrology—and you were the only one to make a heavy killing. That adds up to no mean trick even for a seasoned speculator, let alone someone who'd never touched the market before—and we've no record of you as a participant in any other transaction. Even your broker admitted he'd never heard of you, except as a kid in college." He shifted in the rocker to improve the field of view. Marla shifted also, microscopically; Danny could not tell exactly what the resultant of the two movements would be, but he was all the same prepared to swear that the FBI man's attention was not entirely on his job—and that the diversion was not buying the operative one single square millimeter more visibility than Marla thought necessary.

He was inexplicably pleased. "This is all as circumstantial as I've ever heard," he said. "If I've committed any crime, please name it. Otherwise I've other fish to fry."

The FBI man laughed gently, still without bothering to look at Danny. "Smart operators rarely commit overt crimes," he said. "Sometimes we even have to tag them for violation of the Sherman Act. When we can't do that, we subpoena them as material witnesses."

"Witnesses to what?"

"Why, violation of the Sherman Act, or the Robinson-Patman Act if we really have to stretch a point. Weren't you listening?"

"About as much as you were looking."

86

"Tcha. I'm sorry, Mr. Caiden. Your young lady is handsome; you should be flattered."

Danny kept his hands at his sides with difficulty. The distracted agent's sardonic chatter had begun to make sense, and he needed to know as exactly as possible where he stood. Certainly the fact that the Attorney General's office had planned to keep the indictment a secret until the official announcement was crucial; without Danny's premature revelation in the pages of the *Chronicler*, the indictment could have had no prior effect upon the market.

The further fact that the toboggan in the value of IW's stock had found one sole investor—himself—already undercutting the company to the exact level of its devaluation would smell to the rest of the Street, and to the government, like deliberately induced panicking, under orders from IW itself. Similar tactics had been used in the Zaharoff and Insull scandals.

But Danny, unlike Samuel Insull, wasn't an old and repentant exile, and couldn't expect to get the sob-sister treatment in the consumer dailies—or, as Taylor liked to dub them, the "wypers." If it should turn out that Wheat actually had planned to manipulate the market against the indictment the firm must have known was coming, Danny would be the goat, and it would be as big a surprise to IW as it would be to Danny. He would be flayed alive promptly by the curb-market wolves.

Precognition, it would appear, had blown another fuse.

"Are you arresting me, then?" he said dispiritedly.

"Well, temporarily. You've been subpoenaed by a Grand Jury investigating collusion toward price-fixing, violation of SEC and FEC regulations, and possible violations of

87

the Sherman and Robinson-Patman Acts as amended. Legally, you're accused of nothing yet; we just want to know more about you, and we're seeing to it that we find out. So, technically, you're not being arrested. You're simply being detained for questioning."

"Like a bum on a vagrancy charge."

"Yes, if you like. You'll need a lawyer, however; better get one. We're much more interested in you than we would be in a vagrant." The FBI man moved the rocker a little. It didn't seem to do him much good.

"What does it mean in terms of what I can do and can't do?"

"It means that the Grand Jury will want to be able to reach you at this address. That's all. You'll be expected to retain counsel, and to live here until you're called. You'll be called within a few days, I expect, so make sure you don't leave the building without notification. I wouldn't leave it at all if I were you, Mr. Caiden. If you do, you might wind up in a cell. Oh, and by the way: we've already taken steps toward collecting your today's earnings as bond."

"I can't collect my money?"

"No. We aren't at all sure that it's yours to collect. It may belong to quite a few small investors who expected their dough to be handled honestly."

Without warning, and without looking at the FBI man or otherwise moving in any way, Marla said: "What a pack of thieves!"

The FBI man peeped regretfully at her frozen, immovable calves and stood up. "I'm sorry, miss," he said, in a voice which suggested that he might be talking to a human being. "I have to do the job I'm handed to do."

Marla didn't answer. Danny was speechless. The FBI man finally looked at him, not unkindly, but not very interestedly either; the operative's eyes were blind and inexpressive.

"It's not my function to call you guilty or innocent, Mr. Caiden," he said. "You look all right. If you are, your best bet is to stay put. If you break bond, the Grand Jury will take it as evidence of guilt.

"Stick around and fight it out. If you're on the up-and-up, you'll come out on top. The FBI will give you legal help if you can't afford it yourself." He swivelled suddenly and smiled at Marla, but she was still looking out of the black window. "Frankly, I don't see how a man your age could be the evil genius the SEC thinks you are—you simply couldn't have accumulated enough experience. Stick as tight as a cocklebur and you'll be cleared."

"Thanks," Danny said numbly. He had been saying "Thanks" for the most varied favors lately.

"Don't mention it." The agent looked back at Marla, shrugged, and left. The door slammed.

Marla moved then; she stood up and walked over to the window, at which she had been looking the whole time. Danny didn't pause to analyze the change. He reclaimed the big chair gratefully and put his head in his hands.

It had begun to seem to him that he had spent his whole life huddled in that chair, wondering what to do next. Right now the angle of arms, back and cushions was as good as a cul-de-sac. He couldn't leave, and he couldn't stay.

Possibly the landlord could be persuaded to believe that his reasons for wanting Danny to leave had to bow before the FBI's insistence that Danny stay; but, though the probability of success was fairly high, Danny rejected the idea. That way led to still more whispering among the neighbors.

Did you hear? That Mr. Caiden in Five-D had a woman in his apartment, and now the FBI's after him. Says he can't leave the building. Locked him in his room, that's what I heard. I always did think he wasn't quite right in his mind. He reads a lot, that's bad for you, pretty soon you get morbid. And with children in the building, too. Mrs. Schoenbrun says he keeps spiders. I wouldn't put it past him. He's a Communist, if you ask me. Otherwise why would the FBI? A man with his nose in a book all the time, he's bound to be some kind of subversive. It gives them ideas. And such a nice looking young man, too.

Danny wondered distractedly how that last, faintly friendly condemnation had crept into the vividly-imagined conversation. His unconscious was clutching at straws.

But his unconscious wasn't responsible. The conversation continued, after he had already turned his mind to the main subject.

David, be sure to lock the door. He comes home early sometimes and . . .

Danny could guess where that one had come from: the cheap jane across the hall. He clutched frantically at his head. What a hell of a time to develop a telepathic bump!

But it told him that it was already too late. The building knew about the FBI; gossip travels faster than light. If there were housewives on Mars, they were talking about him right now; and talk like that had a way of attracting newspapermen—indeed, any leak from the FBI itself would bring a horde of newsmen down upon him.

This penultimate indignity he would not suffer; he could not remain for it. And he had to see Todd, tomorrow. But he couldn't leave, either. The Grand Jury had forbidden it. And the SEC had impounded his earnings . . .

He felt like a rat in a maze, charged to bursting with desperation, shaken by continuous failures to find where he was expected to go, on the verge of furious and complete nervous collapse. The voices were gone now, but his head ached horribly. The strain of coping with the supernormal and its unpredictable effects upon normality was sucking away his vitality remorselessly, and it would not stop.

The psi faculties were growing in him, growing like any other exercised talent, with practice. Thus far, even Mme. Zaza had been right. But Danny remembered the curt speech of a violin teacher who'd given him up in disgust twenty years ago:

"Practice makes perfect," the teacher had said. "But it can also cut your throat."

The violin teacher had known instinctively something it had taken Korzybski years to sweat out: that all proverbs are Aristotelian, and tell you nothing useful without a modifying second sentence. Even now, after twenty years, he had the goods on Danny. There would be no point in practicing these wild talents if practice didn't lead eventually to better control. If practice was to lead instead only into a continuous chain of catastrophes, Danny should

91

abandon it as finally as he had been forced to abandon the violin.

Except that he didn't know how to do even that little.

Marla turned and looked at him, and there was something oddly gentle in her eyes.

"You *are* in a jam, aren't you?" she said. "It looks like Marla may have backed the wrong horse."

"The window is still open," Danny said listlessly. "Go get your bet back and go home."

She shook her head. "You don't get rid of me now, Danny. I'm staying. Tell me the story."

"Oh, for Christ's sake—"

"No, just to ease up on the pressure. I promise not to believe a single word you say, but you're going to have to get it out or blow a gasket."

Resignedly, Danny told the too-familiar story again, cutting the front end short, partly in weariness and partly in contempt of anything so sleazy going under the name of a story, more practically because there was a three-em add to go on the tail of it since the story had been run through last.

"When I was in high school," he said suddenly, "my folks got caught in a craze called five-suit bridge. It was all over the country for a while, though compared with canasta you'd never have noticed it. It had the usual hearts, clubs, diamonds, spades, and the fifth suit was called 'Eagles.' "

"Crowns," the girl said. "I know the deck; I bought one once. I thought the fifth suit would come in handy for card tricks if I could think up some to use it in, but I never got around to it. It was called 'Crowns.' "

"Maybe so. If it was called 'Crowns' I'll bet money you got your pack before the craze; probably the deck was thought up in Europe and when the craze started some superpatriot thought the game would sell better if it was changed to 'Eagles.' Under any name it was a freak suit, and it didn't last. I thought myself it would have gone better in poker, not straight poker but the complicated kinds you wind up playing when there are women in the game." (*Except this one*, he thought. He could tell by one look that there was not a spit-in-the-ocean, one-eyed-jacks-and-deuces-wild, high-and-low-hand-split-the-pot cell in her body.)

"And you're it," she said.

"You bet I'm it," Danny said. "A low honor, a wild card in a freak suit. The jack of Eagles in person, all things to all men but nothing to himself."

"I still prefer Crowns," Marla said. "I'm glad you told me. I've even got a good moral reason for staying now, now that I see you're really in trouble, if I need it. I like long odds. When they pay off, they pay off like crazy."

"Agh," Danny said. "The hell with that horse talk. I've had my—"

He shut his mouth with an audible snap and stood absolutely still, stunned. "Wait a minute," he said finally. "Wait a minute. I said 'I'll bet money.' But I didn't. I bet horses."

"Is there a difference?"

"Plenty of difference. Rhine's book, the last one, says ESP shows increasing accuracy with increases in the number of things it handles."

"That's great. I don't get it."

"You don't have to. You're still staying? All right, you can be useful. How much money do you have?"

She stiffened with mock alarm. "Wait a minute, Junior. You're talking to Marla now. She's a smart girl, remember? No ponies—that's flat."

He hardly heard her. "Large numbers of identical objects, that's the ticket. Not horses—they're all individuals, all unique combinations. But dollar bills—just alike, travelling mostly in groups of twos, and we'll pay no attention to any other kind of money. We won't fuss with the actual outcomes of races—that's a stiff problem in math, and I'll bet it can't be beaten parapsychologically any more than it can normally. But we can stick to the flow of the money, dollar bills only, across the betting counters."

"You talk nonsense."

"I do?" He grinned ironically at her. "You wanted to learn how I work, didn't you? Well, here's your chance." He dug out one of his remaining bills and gave it to her. "Stick that in your purse, if you've got one. Add whatever you have to it. We won't need the racing forms or the names of individual horses for this trick. Let's see—"

He got up and went to the window, staring blindly through the pane and remembering that spinning of the minute billions over the surfaces of his brain. A second later the memory had merged with reality and his head was buzzing with pain.

He didn't care. He groped for a pencil, hit the washstand instead and his fingers closed on the piece of soap. With a corner of this he scribbled figures on the windowglass.

"Goody. It's Hallowe'en."

"Shut up and pay attention. Place your bets in that order on any horses that show odd-chains in this order; understand? When you get a return of eighteen to one on the fourth bet—and you will—repeat the sixth bet twice. Then repeat the first bet, then wait for a two-to-one return on the ninth bet, like this, and—"

The girl had found the pencil, moistened the end of it and was rubbing the figure-chains on the window into the fabric of her handkerchief. "I'm not a moron, I can follow the numbers. If you keep chattering I'll make a mistake in copying them."

"All right."

She threw the pencil down on the telephone table. "There. I don't know why I'm doing this, you understand, but it's a cinch it isn't love."

She stuffed Danny's money casually into her purse and slipped out the door. Briefly Danny wondered if he'd ever see her again, but with an immediate and placid certainty which had nothing to do with the fact that the present take would be too small to satisfy her.

Then he forgot her at once, a lapse which would have astonished him had he been aware of it. Suddenly he was pawing frantically through the library books he had brought home, flipping pages with a speed which even he would have said would make it impossible to see what was on them, or stopping suddenly to read a paragraph or four pages in a row or a single line, in no order and by no plan which he could discern. The tiny things were still flowing like fire over the convolutions of his brain, which he took as an earnest of some kind of guidance.

Under the goad of that cruel supersensory librarian he

discarded Tyrrell's book at once, though the rational part of his mind protested at it. The work was jammed with important information, but little of it was germane to the immediate problem. He did not know how he knew, but he knew. The new Rhine book he had already read, and besides, he could depend upon Todd to take care of that end of the business. Littleton gave him one case history which he read with fanatic intensity—unaware that all he had actually done was to slow his paging down to about a page every two seconds until he had gone past the section—and several more which applied marginally to what he was seeking. The Houdini book, as he had suspected, was useless.

It was *An Experiment With Time* which finally put him on the track. He stood up with a shock of alarm when he hit the crucial chapter, remembering how close he had come to missing the Dunne book altogether, then had to sit down again for sheer dizziness. Then came the two Ouspenskii works, both massive, both loaded with incredibly naïve occultism, both—especially the later one, which he had had in his own small library for over a year without touching—paying off. Anyone watching Danny turn pages now would have concluded that he was living at some time-rate from which humans would have seemed virtually immobile, like an insect or a sparrow.

He snatched up the phone and yelled Dr. Todd's home phone number at the operator. After a while Todd's voice answered, very sleepily. Danny talked, grabbing for breath only when he had to and regardless of any sane punctuation. He had been going about two minutes when Todd's own voice began to crackle like frying bacon.

96

"Wait a minute, Danny, you're outrunning me. You read all those books just in the last hour?"

"No, not all of them, just some of them, others I read at the library and anyhow I didn't read all of them through just looked through them for dope, but I'm sure I've got it."

"So am I. I know those books well. The proportion of trash to straight information is terrifically high. If you got this much out of them in one hour or five hours, you must have 'looked through' them as thoroughly as a thousand-volt X-ray. Does your head ache?"

"Why—yes. Pretty badly, now that you mention it."

Todd chuckled unsympathetically. "I thought so. Another subcortical area come into play. You didn't read those books at all—you imprinted their contents on your memory by ESP, and didn't even know you were doing it. All right, Danny, I'll be over at once. Have you got a pencil handy?"

Danny made a brief frantic search of his pockets, saw the pencil lying beside the telephone, and found the point broken. He took the phone over to the dark window, rubbed away the figures on it with his sleeve and picked up the scrap of soap.

"Shoot."

Rapidly Todd dictated a list of equipment. Danny scrawled it on the panes. "All that can come from Otto Meiner's except the encephalograph. For that, you call BA 7-8333 and be sure to tell them who wants it. Your horse trick should pay off, Danny, and that's what we'll use for money. If it doesn't, call me again and—no, I'll be there by that time. Well, I'll have the stuff shipped over from the University in that event. But if we can buy new equipment it'll help."

"The Heisenberg principle?"

"Exactly. In physics the equipment effects the results. In paraphysics the experimenter also effects the equipment. But let's not waste time talking about it on the phone, Danny. We may have the whole answer before morning."

"Right," Danny said. He put the phone back into its cradle and rifled his desk for another pencil. It didn't seem to contain one, but he did find a 27¢ ballpoint pen which he had previously decided would write *only* under water; somehow, he made it do. He had just finished copying the list off the windowpanes when someone struck the door three heavy, magisterial blows.

Gritting his teeth, he threw the door open, and found himself staring at an enormous expanse of color out of which he could at first make no sense at all. Only when he looked farther up did the mass take on any form.

The man in the doorway was about six feet seven inches tall, and the only perfectly oval human being Danny had ever seen. He had vast, deep hips and thighs like an elephant's, which dwindled so steadily and at such an increasing angle to quite small—or, at least, normal-sized —feet that it looked like a trick of perspective. His trunk, too, was largest around the abdomen, his chest only usual and his shoulders narrow, though with forearms which were thick with either muscle or fat or both. The body wore a faded red cummerbund into which a dirty fluorescent violet blouse had been tucked, and aloft a swarthy head of ridiculously inadequate proportions wobbled

98

down at him, bound around with a blue and red bandanna knotted at the back.

The apparition glared at him, and then roared suddenly in a blurred voice:

"Where is sister mine?"

My God, Danny thought, what a family. "She's not here," he said. "Don't shout, you'll wake the neighbors."

The huge man stalked into the room, jostling Danny out of the way with the clumsy effortlessness of an elephant ignoring a tree-branch. "She is to here," he roared. Danny shut the door. "From Mama Zaza I have it, who sneeze before she said, showing it is how true. Has been no lie in family ours two t'ousand years. Where?"

"She's not here, I tell you. She was here, all right, but she left."

"You hurt, I break," the giant said, slightly less loudly. "She come here, she come back maybe. I wait."

What a pack of natural-born squatters! Danny scratched his head. It was difficult to take the comic-opera figure seriously, yet the man was obviously physically powerful and despite his impossible appearance might be the most direct threat Danny had encountered yet. How was he going to get rid of him?

"I don't think she'll be back," he said carefully. "I didn't want her here in the first place. She came of her own accord."

"I wait," the giant said heavily and as if he had not heard. He exhaled a sour miasma of garlic and cheap wine.

"All right," Danny said. "If you wait, you wait. Could you use a drink to pass the time?"

"Hah?"

99

"I said, do you want a drink? You look like you've been without one for quite a while, and maybe she'll be a long time."

"I drink. Bring."

"I can't bring, I've none in the house." Danny hoped the Recording Angel was asleep. "I'll tell you what. You go get some for both of us. There's a good bar around the corner—"

"You go, bring. I wait."

"I can't. I have to answer the telephone. Here." He searched his pockets again, finally remembering that in his shirt pocket there was still a bill. He did not look at it, certain that it was far too small and playing for a delay of that discovery on the giant's part until it was too late. "You take this to the bar and get us a couple of bottles of good wine. You can watch the apartment all the time you're over there if you're afraid I'll run out on you, so you can see Marla come back, if she does. How's that?"

The giant fumbled for words, blinked, and took the money. "You stay," he said threateningly.

"Sure, I'll stay. Go on, I'm getting thirsty."

The giant went out. Danny closed the door, waiting until the creature was out of earshot, and sprang the lock. The lock, of course, would do no real good, for the giant could raise no end of hell simply by battering for admission; but it was Danny's bet that the man would not discover until he was in the bar that the money he had been given was scarcely enough for one, let alone two—and that cunning would prompt him to drink it up before returning.

Considering the load the giant already seemed to be
100

carrying, it ought to be enough; but it was a risk. Marla's brother carried a lot of flesh, and it would take a lot of alcohol to saturate it.

There was a sharp sound at the door, as if somebody had kicked it, not viciously, but only with the intent of opening it. Danny sighed and opened the lock again.

"The next disaster," he said pleasantly, "arrives in ten minutes on Track Four."

chapter eight

~~~~~~

MONEY

It was Marla. Her pocketbook bulged and the pockets of her dress made bumps all over her. Her expression was one of wild exhilaration.

"I'm sold," she said. "Boy, am I sold. And without a race-track open anywhere in this part of the country, too. I just put the money down and followed your figures and now I'm a rich woman. I'm going to buy myself all the illusions ever made, up to and including the Indian Rope Trick."

"The hell you are. Incidentally, I just met a relative of yours."

"What? My aunt? Did she come here?"

"No, your brother. He was looking for you. He was sort of violent about it."

"Oh, God, him. That's not my brother. That's Zaza's son. It's a shakedown they try to work every time they find out where to locate any man I go with. That's one reason I cleared out of Zaza's. Did he get any money out of you?"

"How could he have? I was lucky to have a buck to give him to get drunk on."

She grinned nastily. "That was smart. He'll do it, too. Well, if he comes back here I'll deal with the bastard."

"You won't have the chance. I've got another job for you. Take the dough out again to Otto Meiner's."

"What's that?"

"It's a scientific supply house at the corner of Edgerton and Fifth across the river. They'll be closed, of course, but they have an emergency bell. Tell them Dr. Todd from the University sent you. His secretary will confirm it. When they let you in, buy everything on this list and come back here with it in their truck."

Marla glared at him, her bosom taxing the severe tailored jacket. "Do you mean to send me across the river at this time of night?" she demanded. "Don't you know there's only one ferry running now?"

"Certainly I know it," Danny snapped. "I didn't ask you here in the first place. If you want to learn anything from me you'll earn it. Oh—and leave me about half of that bankroll. You won't need any more."

"Scrooge! All right—here. If I catch my death of cold I'll haunt you."

She went out again. Danny picked up the phone and called the number Todd had given him. A gentle voice, that of a man in whose blood culture was as vital and innate as hemoglobin, tired, but pleasant, answered at once.

"I'm calling for Dr. Todd."

"I know you are," said the voice. "Nobody but Toddy would be sure I'd be here this late. How may I help you?"

"I'm to get a model EU encephalograph, six channels, on emergency order."

103

"This is the place to do that. Shall I bill Todd, the University, or you?"

"Bill me; you can ship it C.O.D.," Danny said. He gave the voice the address. "How much is it?"

"That's a problem. We raised our prices at the end of the month, but I'd better give you the old price, since it's for the good doctor. Call it $2700."

Danny nearly dropped the phone. He counted the money he had. "How would it do," he said at last, "if I paid half now and half later?"

"It will do perfectly. I'll send it to you in half an hour— and if I know Todd, by two in the morning he'll have it half apart and the other half frying eggs. Anything more?"

"No, that's all," Danny said, grinning. "And thank you."

"Oh, you're welcome; glad to get orders, you know. Good night."

Danny hung up somewhat dazedly. That had been his first encounter with that rarest of all the species, the naturally polite human being, in years. If Todd's name alone was as great a power as it seemed with the owner of the voice, then Todd was even more remarkable a man than Danny had suspected.

Now Danny had nothing to do but sit and sweat it out. His researches with the books, spectacular though the results had been in some ways, had reached the limits of his knowledge. Now it was up to Todd to make it work.

The long waiting period gave him plenty of time to remember that he hadn't eaten since breakfast. Drug stores had all been closed for half an hour, but after five phone calls he found an all-night hash joint which was willing to send up half a dozen liverwursts-on-rye. Then he sat down in the big chair again and chewed distractedly on the balky pen.

In half an hour exactly, the encephalograph arrived. It consisted mainly of a longish, waist-high cabinet, on wheels, with two different faces full of controls, and writer units on top. The cabinet itself seemed to be steel, with a green crackle finish. Danny inspected it with the greatest curiosity, and tried to read the operating instructions which came with it, but his knowledge of electronics was entirely too rudimentary to cope with it.

Todd, the remaining equipment and the sandwiches all arrived at once. The equipment came in a two-and-a-half ton truck with Marla perched on its rear, swinging her electrifying legs over the tailgate. Todd watched her from the soap-scrawled window while Danny doled out his silver to the boy from the hash joint.

"And here's another two bucks," Danny said. "One of them is for you. The other one is for a big character wearing a bandanna and a red sash, who's getting blotto in the bar across the street. After you give it to him, come back here and tell me what shape he's in and I'll give you another buck."

"Yes, *sir*," the boy said.

"Is that your girl, Danny? She's a pretty thing." Todd looked interested.

"I never saw her before today," Danny said, chewing busily. "But I can safely say that she's become attached to me. She thinks I'm a charlatan and wants to find out how I do it, so she can become one herself."

Todd smiled. "Well, with luck she'll find out—providing she can understand it. I see Henry got the EEG to you."

105

"You mean that thing? Yes. Who is he, by the way?"

"He's Rahm's president; a brilliant physicist and one of the hardest-working men I ever encountered in my life."

"He must be hard working, to be at it this late," Danny said. "Scientists don't get to be company presidents very often, I imagine."

"No, but Henry's not the usual kind of scientist, nor the usual kind of anything else, either. Hello, there's the next instalment."

The driver stood patiently while Todd read the markings on the crate. "That's the resonator. Better put that on the bed. I want to assemble it in a chain of steps, and there won't be room enough on the table."

Marla came in with a smaller package, breathing heavily and glaring bloody murder at Danny. "What'll I do with this?"

"Put it on the desk for the moment," Danny said. "Marla, this is Dr. Todd from the University. Relax and have a sandwich. We're going to be up all night."

"I'm already resigned to it," the girl sighed. She watched interestedly while Danny and Todd unpacked. A small transformer was plugged into a wall socket and from it Todd swiftly rigged a bewildering network of step-down leads.

The last item from the truck was the biggest—an operating chair, such as surgeons use for working on the brain. It looked very much like a dentist's chair, or did until Todd mounted the electrode box from the encephalograph on it. The EEG cabinet itself he wheeled against the far wall, at right angles to the chair, at the fullest extension of the instrument's input cable.

"This thing has rejection circuits against 60-cycle interference, but I think I'd better shield that transformer all the same," Todd muttered. "At least we won't have to shield the patient, though. That's you, Danny."

Rewiring the standard lie-detector took longer, and no police technician would have recognized it when Todd was through with it.

"That'll do for a start," Todd said finally. "We'll make more changes as the need arises."

"All right, Dr. Todd, just a second," Danny said. The boy from the hash joint was at the door again. "Did you find the guy?"

"No, sir," the boy said. "The barkeep said he was there and got into a fight with a guy and got pitched out. He said he was fighting drunk."

"Oh, oh," Danny said. "I don't like the sound of that. Okay, my friend, you get the dollar that was for him, and thanks."

"Right—thanks yourself, mister."

"He'll be back," Marla said darkly.

"Nothing that I can do about it, Marla. What's first, Dr. Todd?"

"Well, first let's get the record straight on this telekinetic trick," Todd said. "Tell me just what the sensation was."

Danny explained, as well as he could, the whirling sensation and the pain that went with it. When he got to the levitation of the table in the medium's parlor, Todd's eyes were sparkling.

"That's the Blackett effect," he said. "You cut down the gravitational field of every atom in that table. Sheer centrifugal force from the Earth's rotation put the table aloft, and Coriolis forces from the same source made it crawl along the ceiling. A beautiful demonstration of something that's been only speculation up to now."

"Atoms? Then the whirling things—"

"Are electrons, of course. I think we won't need to use a bit of this equipment to give you full conscious control of PK at least. All we need to do is implant full conscious understanding of the physical process in your cortex, and the last connection will be opened. To start with, I suppose you know what centrifugal force is. How about Coriolis force?"

"That's like centrifugal, except that it makes an object in revolution crawl sidewise instead of outward."

"Just so. The force that made water splash in Mr. Newton's whirling bucket. Now then—" He pulled an envelope from his jacket pocket, scribbled rapidly on it, and shoved the result under Danny's nose. "Here, look at this."

The paper said: $G = (2CP/BU)^2$. Danny looked at it.

"I don't feel any different," he confessed.

"Do you know what magnetic moment is?"

Danny tried to bring back his college physics. "Let's see—it's, uh, the product of the strength of a magnetic charge and the distance between the poles?"

"Right. You have a mind like a steel trap, Danny; you've been wasting your substance in journalism. Now look back at the equation. Magnetic moment is what P stands for. U stands for angular momentum, G is the universal gravitational constant, and C is the invariant velocity of light. What I'm out to show you is that a magnetic field is a product of rotation on an axis, and that gravity is a function of it. Now if you'll remember that every electron is a tiny electromagnet, and figure in B as an uncertainty correction amounting to about zero point twenty-five—"

Danny strained to put the factors together, with a mind long unaccustomed to the kind of rigorously orderly handling of symbols required even by simple algebra. Todd watched him with narrowed, eager eyes.

Pop.

Suddenly, just like that, he saw it. The figures, really, didn't matter. It was the relationship that counted. He blinked inadvertently with astonishment.

Todd's answering smile was almost predatory. "Move something," the scientist suggested.

The cake of soap, which had been leading a remarkably adventurous life during the past three hours, shot off the window sill across the room in a flat trajectory, smashed against the opposite wall and dropped into the innards of the resonator. Part of it remained sticking to the wallpaper.

Todd went over and fished the free piece out of the apparatus on the bed. "Take it easy," he said, chuckling. "You'll gain control with practice. In the meantime, use a little less power than you think is necessary. You had the gain cranked up enough that time to throw a lead pig."

"What I still don't understand," Danny said, "is where the juice comes from. Just understanding the process can't be enough—it takes an actual expenditure of energy to move a cake of soap, whether you use psychokinesis or just pick it up by hand and give it the old-fashioned heave ho."

109

"You're expending energy, Danny," Todd said calmly. "And plenty of it. PK appears to be one of the highest forms of activity of the human brain, and you'll find it extremely tiring if you keep at it for long stretches. The electrons you affect first are your own, in the cells of your own brain. You project the resulting field onto the object you want to move, since obviously you don't want to teleport the insides of your skull. Result: levitation."

"Then you should be able to do it, Dr. Todd."

"I've been trying for the past two hours," Todd said, with calm regret. "I can't summon up the initial sensation, the movement of electrons inside my own head. Nothing happens, that's all; I'm afraid I haven't the talent."

Danny felt inexplicably guilty. What right had he to be gaining mastery over this power after so little study, when a man with ten times his intelligence and years of careful study was denied it?

"Don't worry," Todd said, exactly as if he were telepathic. "I'm a teacher, not a doer, and I know it. Let's get on with it; we've only just begun."

Danny turned his head suddenly and looked at Marla. She was standing with her back against the door, watching him with wide eyes. She had one fist crammed in her mouth.

"What's the matter, Marla? Isn't this what you wanted to see? Does it scare you?"

She removed the fist with difficulty; obviously it took courage for her to move at all.

"You bet it does," she said. "It just hit me that you might really not have been kidding. I mean when you

110

said you didn't fake this business. If so, I don't like it worth a damn. It isn't natural."

"Of course it's natural," Todd scoffed. "People who've never managed to think farther than a mile from their own egos feel the same way about light-years, Marla, but that doesn't make interstellar distances unnatural. It just makes them unfamiliar. Now, Danny, climb into the chair and let's get started on ESP. I warn you that it will be harder come by, because we've good reason to suppose that it's partly nonphysical." He filled a syringe from a rubber-capped vial and jutted the needle out at Danny's forearm. "Roll up your sleeve and we'll start the tracer process rolling while we work."

"What are you going to do now?" Marla said warily.

"Check an idea of Danny's," Todd said, smearing Danny's temples and a spot on his forehead with acetone in a cotton pad. Danny sat down in the surgeon's chair, and Todd began to apply a gray goo—SS electrode compound—to the spots on Danny's scalp which he had just cleaned, using a tongue depressor with deft strokes. "Danny suggested to me that the activity of the psi mechanism as a whole may be that of an infinitely overlapping group of Fourier functions, in which the nerve-impulses play the part of dynamical variables."

"Hey, take it easy. Give it to me in English."

Danny smiled. "I don't recognize it stated that way either, Marla. All I proposed was that the unused part of the human brain might not share the one-way view of time that the gray matter is used to. The so-called 'arrow of time,' which points forward only, is a sort of myth that we grow up with; people didn't always think of

111

time that way. The Greeks, for instance, thought of themselves as travelling *backwards* through time, with new events coming into view in the present just as objects come into view from behind when you're riding backwards in a train. Some American Indian families or tribes don't think of time in terms of past and future at all, but only in terms of some kind of ever-changing present that it's difficult for our minds to grasp—just because we weren't raised in that attitude. Do you follow me so far?"

"I think I do. But I don't see what it's got to do with being clairvoyant."

"It has everything to do with it. None of these ways of looking at time is a total way, a realistic way, as I understand it. Actually, all events—past, present, and future—exist together. They don't just flash into being in some mythical present and then flash out of existence again when the present magically becomes the past. They only seem to, because the observer's consciousness is moving among them and hits them only one at a time.

"What I suggested to Dr. Todd was: the psi mechanism of the brain can sense all this, and acts upon it directly; while the gray matter, the cortex of the brain, is blinded to it by prescientific ways of looking at things. Dr. Todd's formulation a moment ago is a mathematical way of putting that idea which I don't understand any more than you do—and I don't see why we should have to. That's what he's here for."

The girl thought about it. "If I make any sense out of that at all," she said finally, "you're saying that all events are fixed, and have to happen the way they do happen. Predestination."

112

"That's the cortical way of looking at it," Todd said, snapping the encephalograph electrodes into the gray goo and painting their upper sides with deft swipes of his tongue depressor. "If you're going to insist on thinking in those terms, then I suppose you'll have to call it pre-destination. But it's not a rigid, linear series, with events falling 1-2-3-4 like beads on a string.

"Dunne, for instance, envisages an infinite series of overlapping event-levels, every one of them keyed to some sort of decision-point. Plenty of room for operation of free will there, you see, if you have to be comforted by such an essentially metaphysical conceit."

"Ouch!" Marla said ruefully. "I can't help it if I'm a layman, Dr. Todd. Is it all right if I think of it as a big pile of movie films, all stacked lengthwise on top of each other? They all have almost exactly the same sets in the pictures, but the frames all overlap each other a bit, and the leading character has permission to shift from strip to strip if he likes. At least that's what I get from what you say."

"That's a very good way to think of it," Todd said gravely. He plugged in the electrodes to the electrode box, crossed the room, and began to calibrate the encephalograph. "I'm none too sure of your Poisson-brackets anyhow, Danny. I think we might better assume that your impulse-groups correspond to Heisenberg's 'probability packets.' Marla's analogy would apply better there, too."

"Whatever you like; you're the boss on the heavy thinking," Danny said, resettling himself in the chair, which was none too comfortable. "That's what we've got to find out, of course. What Dr. Todd wants to do, Marla,

H   113 is check that idea and find out whether or not it's even close to the actual ESP function. Then, if it does turn out to be the right track, he needs to localize the psi centers in my brain, and put them under my conscious control. That's what all this apparatus is for."

"Ready, Danny."

The encephalograph hummed, almost inaudibly. On a slowly travelling, heat-sensitive paper, six heated-point styli drew complicated traces. Todd watched their movements critically.

"What are you trying to do, compose a limerick?" he asked. "Relax, Danny, I can't make a thing out of that."

"Can the machine tell you what he's thinking?" Marla said incredulously.

"No, of course not. Shush now, girl. Danny, relax. Make like a moron. I want basic patterns first, not something I'd have to call in a cryptographer to read."

Danny closed his eyes and tried to think of nothing at all. Since he was conscious, he could not, of course, succeed completely. But he did manage to empty his mind of everything but fugitive images and washes of faded, unticketable emotions over which he had no control.

"That's better," Todd said. "Just hold that a minute. Shush everybody . . . All right. Now I'll be quiet again in a moment, and then when you're relaxed completely, you lift that chunk of soap again—no, no, Danny, don't visualize it. I don't want the trace messed up with sub-optical activity. Just lift the soap when I say 'When.'"

"How can I, without visualizing it?"

"You don't have to visualize it. Your psi mechanism

114

is in direct physical contact with it. Now relax again. . . .
Good. . . . *Hoist!*"

Danny hoisted. Todd grunted with satisfaction, and
Danny's eyes popped open involuntarily. The soap fell
straight down from a position high above the desk.

Todd was holding an X-ray plate just over his forehead,
with rock-steady hands.

"Don't be impatient. There's a long way to go yet.
I want more of these, and then a series of plates from
the sides, the back, and off the top of the skull. Shut your
eyes."

Danny shut his eyes. Todd repeated the procedure;
then again; and again, and again. Danny discovered that
he was falling asleep.

"Good, very good. Take a break, Danny." Danny's eyes
flew open. Todd was slipping his plates into the sink
and covering them with Danny's scatter rug.

"You haven't any fluid in your developing bath,"
Marla's voice said sleepily.

"I don't need fluid. There's an ammonia-soaked sponge
in there. Those are xerograms—dry-plates." The scientist
began to lock Danny's wrists down to the arms of the
chair, and wheeled the converted lie-detector into position.

"Now, Marla, let's be tee-totally quiet for an hour
or so. Every word you say registers with Danny, and
makes my kymographs wiggle. We don't need that kind
of data. This is the crucial stage. Now then, children,
softly, softly. Shush."

Danny closed his eyes. The quiet became absolute.

He dreamed that he was . . .

No. That was irrevocable. No. But it was already too late. He had done it out of curiosity and it was too late to learn from it. It was too late. No, no, no, no . . .

He gasped and tried to sit up, but his wrists were strapped. Faint light was coming in through the window; dawn.

"All right, Danny," Todd's voice said huskily. "We're about through now."

Danny looked around under gummy eyelids. Marla was frankly and unequivocally asleep in the armchair. The scientist, only a shadow, was studying the latest in the interminable series of plates, his movements deliberately monotonous. As Todd held the new plate before the lamp, Danny saw on it a pattern that looked like the bursting of a skyrocket. It seemed to satisfy Todd profoundly. There was an air of sternly repressed excitement about him.

"Danny, wake up."

"Um." The light in the room disappeared. Evidently it was not yet dawn; the light had been an illusion, born from Danny's flight from his nightmare. (*No, no* . . . but it was over, it really was over.) "What time is it?"

"About five. Are you awake?"

"Sort of. Got anything?"

"Yes. The Fourier idea was right, after all. It looks to me as if the whole ESP center is in operation now; but there still aren't any impulse traces through to your cortex. I want you to see how much of an event-series you can pick up, say, five minutes from now. Anything at all. My movements in the room, or anything that might be going on in the street."

116

"Aw ri—" Danny struggled with his semi-stupor, evading the traces of the nightmare. Todd's glance shot to the paper strip travelling evenly over the top of the encephalograph.

"Don't," he said hoarsely. "Relax again, Danny. Go back to sleep if you can. I want your cortex nearly cut out. Softly now . . ."

Danny slumped obediently in the torture chair. Thin currents of apprehension wove through him; his mind was drifting over an abyss which he thought he recognized. After a while, there were dim shapes superimposed upon the familiar geography of the room. He moved protestingly.

"Danny?"

"Um. Getting something. No movement, though."

"Probably just one 'frame,' to use Marla's analogy. See if you can expand the reference-points."

He was not conscious of trying; he wasn't sure that he understood what had been asked of him. But, without volition, the dim figures which he sensed in the room began to move. At the same time, a section of the street outside, including a frontal slice of the apartments below his, became directly sensible. It was an odd and dizzying perception for which no words existed.

He felt a vague sense of alarm, less horrifying than the nightmare had been, but much more real.

"I'm estanning—" he murmured.

"You're what? I can't quite hear you."

"I didn't mean that. Dr. Todd, something I don't like here. Something wrong. More people in the room than I can account for. There's Marla and you and there's me

117

in the chair, but there's another figure by the window—and now he's moving and there's another guy who seems to be falling, and—and also there's a car downstairs with two more people in it. Some kind of a fracas. It—it smells funny, that's the only way I can describe it."

Todd was watching the converted lie detector like a spectacled hawk; the little pens scratched busily away, making traces which only he could read. "Go on."

"I've lost it," Danny said. "No, wait—a couple of these birds have guns. Now there's a scramble. And—no, there it goes again." He opened his eyes and sat forward in the chair, fully awake now. "What do you make of that?"

Todd began to unstrap him. "Nothing I like," he said grimly. "Any chance of localizing the time?"

"Marla will still be here, and so will you. At least I think so. But I couldn't get it clearly. Identities kept getting shuffled. Cripes. What a dream I had."

"I switched polarities on you about an hour ago; that was probably what was responsible. Was it bad? I was a little afraid of it."

"If you really caused it," Danny said bleakly, "I may decide to strangle you where you stand. But I'm getting over it."

Below, a car purred to a stop at the curb. With a quick sweep of his hand, Todd yanked the light cord from its socket, plunging the room into darkness. If there had been any dawn coming, it would have shown now, but the window was still a flat sheet of ink. Danny pulled the electrodes from his head and went over to it.

"Already," he murmured. "See—that first bird's got a tommy gun. Something tells me my manipulations have
118

blown the all-time fuse. I wish I had a sidearm of some kind."

Todd shook Marla.

"Get up, girl. Quick. Danny, show her where your closet is and make her hide in it."

"What's up?" the girl said sleepily.

"Trouble," Danny said. "Come over here, Marla, and get in. Not a peep out of you no matter what you hear."

The doorbell rang, the sharp sound making them all jump. Danny closed the door on Marla.

"Let 'em get in by themselves," Danny said grimly. "I don't think I'm at home. Hadn't we better make some of this equipment safe?"

"Too late and not necessary," Todd summarised tersely. "Damn. Another five minutes and we'd have had the whole story on record. Well, let them stumble over the apparatus and tangle in the spaghetti."

There were fumbling sounds. In the dim ceiling glow from the streetlamp, Danny could see the scientist hefting the small transformer. A blow from a corner of that could crack the toughest skull. Danny grinned, picked up a straight chair and stationed himself behind the door.

"Caiden?" a quiet, harsh voice said. Danny didn't answer. "We know you're in there. We mean business. Open up, or we'll spray the room."

Danny hesitated. He had no idea what the men outside wanted with him; but he knew he didn't dare to take any chances. Machine-gun bullets would surely go through the closet door as well—it was directly in the line of fire.

"All right," he said. "Hold on."

119

He put down the chair, unlocked the door and swung it open.

A powerful flashlight beam flooded the room, catching Todd flatfooted.

"Hello, grampa. Drop that thing. Give us some light here, and snap to it."

Grudgingly, Todd plugged the lamp cord back in. Three men came in, two of them prodding Danny back and taking up stations where they could cover the entire room. One of them was the waiter Danny had seen in the bookie joint.

"Whaddaya know," the waiter said. "This guy was in Joe's place yesterday, boss. No, day before yesterday. He must of been casing us."

"Where's the girl?" the man with the flashlight said.

"What girl?"

"Your runner. We traced her here after that mess she made of the parimutuels tonight."

"She's gone home," Danny said. "She's just a messenger."

"Eddie, you was supposed to of had your eye glued on this place until the boys showed up."

"It has a back door, boss," the waiter said. "I ain't two guys at once."

The man with the flashlight considered it, his eyes roving over the scattered equipment.

After a moment he bent curiously over the plates on the table.

At the same moment Todd, who had unobtrusively retained the transformer throughout, threw it and flung himself flat on the floor. A tommy gun clattered on the boards, its owner toppling like a felled tree.

120

Danny kicked the man with the flashlight expertly and with great force and threw himself in a flying tackle at the remaining gunman.

There was a muffled crash of glass and the bursting of tubes as the headman lunged, flailing, over the encephalograph, which rolled out from under him and smacked against the sink. Danny had no chance to keep track of him. The man he had tackled, seemingly unwilling to shoot, was clubbing him furiously with the butt of his gun. Danny heaved and brought him down.

There was a rush of heavy shoes behind him, and then several pairs of hands grabbed him by the arms and threw him away. At least three more men had come in, evidently from posts outside the door. Danny belatedly threw the newly-mastered PK into gear and sent the fallen tommy gun hurtling straight at the nearest one.

The man's mouth dropped open. He was too incredulous to duck. Todd writhed in the grip of a gorilla at least twice his size, kicking him hard in the shins. The man winced, but held on, swearing luridly. A moment later and there were two of them kneeling on Danny.

He got his water tumbler and a heavy dictionary into action. A muzzle ground into the small of his back.

"Quit throwin' stuff around," the harsh voice panted. "I don't care how you do it but the next thing takes off by itself I'll blow you in two."

The sentence was scrambled but its meaning was all too clear. Danny subsided obediently, and the assorted objects he had had whistling around the room dropped inertly to the floor.

121

"What'll we do with the old geezer, boss?"

"Truss him up and stick him in the closet. This guy's the smart joker that's been the cause of the trouble. Use some of that there wire."

The gorilla wound Todd with wire until he resembled an electronic-age mummy. When he opened the closet door, Danny's umbrella slammed over his head.

"Cripes, another one! Grab her, Tooey. So you didn't go home after all, sister? Wire her up, Tooey."

In the hall, someone said, "What the hell—" and there was a flat smack. Another gunman staggered backward into the room. After him rolled a mountain in full quake.

"You have sister mine! I break you all—"

With the perfect, idiot precision of a machine, Tooey's barrel chest swivelled where he was crouching beside Marla, the automatic glided out of his jacket and blared. Danny could clearly hear both impacts of the bullet— once against the giant's chest, once more in the wall of the stairwell behind him. The drunken gypsy fell backward, his face blind and furious, utterly unaware that it was dead.

"Jesus. What is this, a mob or a UN meeting? All right, let's beat it. Throw some water on them two dummies and wake 'em up. People live in these kind of joints is awful nosey—one of 'em'll of called the cops by now."

Bound and gagged, Todd and Marla were stood in opposite corners of the closet and the door closed in their faces. Danny tried to project some kind of reassurance, but any telepathic bump he might have had obstinately refused to function. Since neither Todd nor Marla were

122

telepaths, and since the reassurance was mythical any-how, he knew he could have expected nothing else.

He was jerked to his feet, and something nudged his ribs.

"March."

chapter nine

~~~~~~

TETHER'S END

For the first twenty minutes Danny concentrated care-fully upon marking the course the heavy car took through the early morning. The few scraps of conversation ex-changed by his captors only served to confirm his first impression of them.

They were hired hoods, most of them, under the lead-ership of small-time gamblers attached to a sizeable syndicate. No purpose would be served by learning to tell these small fry apart. The identity of the man he was being taken to see might be a matter of more importance.

The car had just swung onto the upper reaches of the Kingsway Bridge when Danny realized that the driver was making no effort to confuse him. Thus far he could plot their course from the apartment as easily as if he had left a chalk-line. They had followed the quickest and most direct route out of the city, the same one that the Chamber of Commerce recommended to tourists.

The lesson was plain.

They didn't expect Danny to be coming back.

Five minutes into the country away from the bridge, the car shot down a long, curving gravel drive and pulled up. The house that was their destination was long and low, and could have been anything from a disreputable roadhouse to an abandoned country home. Danny was hustled around to the back without being given a chance to see the main entrance.

"Here he is, chief," the man with the flashlight said. Danny was shoved roughly into a small, thickly carpeted room, most of which was taken up by a heavy glass-topped desk. The man behind the desk was expensively dressed, but unimpressive, with the small build and terrier face of an undernourished Irishman. Danny had never seen him before.

"Shut the door, Tooey. So you're Danny Caiden. Your mother must of hung too much around the movies."

"The name's a corruption of a New Orleans term that would be familiar to anybody with two brain cells," Danny said evenly. "What's your name?"

"I'm asking the questions," the man behind the desk said. "Murph, are you sure this is the guy?"

"Yeah. We found the girl that passed the money hidin' in a closet. And him and an old geezer and a big guy tried to jump us."

"The way you guys probably came at them that wouldn't prove nothing."

"Eddie says the guy was in Joe's day before yesterday, casing the place," Murph said surlily. "He's the guy, all right."

"All right. Everybody clear out but Tooey."

"Look," Danny said. "I'm a law-abiding citizen, or I

125

was until you guys snatched me. Now I'm violating my bond. I don't know what cause you've got to be mad at me—I didn't do anything in Joe's but lose all my dough."

"No? Maybe not. But what you did last night was pretty tricky. You won't get away with playing dumb, Caiden. No one but a guy who knew to the last dollar how we had things rigged could have loused us up the way you did. Hell, I know exactly how every race on our tracks is supposed to go today, but even knowing that much I couldn't ruin the odds the way you did.

"I figure you cost the syndicate about twenty-five grand." He crossed his arms on the glass and leaned forward. "And I know what your take was, too. Forty-five hundred fish, that's all. Less than a fifth of what you could of made by playing with us instead of against us. That means new competition. *Who are you working for?*"

"Myself," Danny said.

"Don't give me that. Nobody who knows the score is going to take a fifth of the kitty instead of the whole business. And no one man could beat down the odds no matter *what* he knew. He'd have to have touts and markers, not just a girl and an old man and a pug. Who's paying you to louse us up? Who's your boss?"

Danny shrugged. "I don't have any boss. What's it to me what you believe? Take it or leave it."

The man's eyes became still harder. "If you want me to swallow that, you'll have to prove it. If you did this all by yourself you got a system."

"You could call it that."

The racketeer smiled gently. "Explain it," he said.

For a moment the two men looked at each other. Then Danny smiled back.

"All right," he said. "It's not difficult—when you know how. In dealing with the mass behaviour of any indefinitely large number of similar objects—such as electrons or dollar bills—the old Hamiltonian laws of periodic motion don't apply. That is, the variables don't follow the commutative multiplication law.

"In terms of racing, if you ignore the horses and concentrate on the dough, you can describe its motion across the counter as a problem in matrix mechanics—not as a trig series, the way an actuary would go about it." Danny was just as glad Todd wasn't here to listen in. As far as he knew, he was simply quoting Todd, but he was fairly sure he had it distorted somewhere along the line. "You can't follow any individual dollar, but you can say that its position in the betting order can be described at any point as a table of integer differences between value-terms—"

"Tooey," the man behind the desk said. A stunning blow caught Danny just behind the left temple. He lurched to one knee, his head ringing painfully.

"Now maybe we understand each other," the man behind the desk said. "I know all the kinds of double-talk there are, Caiden. A guy once tried to talk me into buying an actuarial system. Now tell me who it is you're working for, before I decide politeness don't pay."

Danny shook his head. The sharp, agonizing ringing continued. The voice of the man behind the desk seemed doubled, somehow, the second section arriving just behind the first like the payoff cars of a crack train. All

127

during his previous speech, the second section was saying:

This is a new one. Wise guy, too. Maybe Joe's—no, he hasn't the nerve. This guy the boss? No such luck. Sweat it out of him before—

He lifted his eyes and looked at the man behind the desk through a fog of pain. The queer, jerky monologue continued, though the man's mouth was shut. Danny recognized the pain then, and it made him sick with hope. Could such a simple thing as a knock on the head have turned the trick? With the psi centers in a state of abnormal excitation from the radio-ekacesium Todd had injected, the blow had apparently completed the job Todd had not been allowed time to finish. Cautiously, Danny reached out for Tooey's mind.

Tooey could hardly be said to have a mind. He had an intricate, delicately-balanced complex of glandular states, capable of being triggered along several limited channels by the slightest thalamic disturbance; but his cortical thoughts, when he had any, were of about the same calibre as the speeches in the balloons of comic strips.

The stream of consciousness of the man behind the desk was of a considerably higher order, but it had its own instabilities. There was fear of deposition in every impulse of it.

"Speak up, you. I don't want to miss my breakfast. I got business. Who's your boss?"

"Joe," Danny said thickly, struggling back to his feet. "I didn't mean any harm. Honest."

The man behind the desk picked up the phone. "Murph? Nab Eddie and put him in cold storage until

128

I can talk to him. And send out a car after Joe." He hung up and looked back at Danny. "Now who gives you the figures?"

Danny thought fast. "I get 'em by mail," he said. "I have to go down to Joe's to check when I take 'em in to be sure there's no mistake. I don't see him. I just make bets like anybody else and he sends me word."

"How?"

"By my wins and losses. If they check out the letter was okay and I go ahead and—"

"All right. Tooey, take him out and get rid of him."

The gorilla's hand descended on Danny's shoulder. The telephone on the desk shrilled. Danny could feel the adrenal surge of alarm wash through the narrow corridors of Tooey's brain, and sensed also the instant hair-trigger adjustment of the man behind the desk.

Tooey's was the usual stupid man's reaction to any modern news-carrying system: the news was always bad to such a mind, because it was always new and hence always an unexpected change. For the man behind the desk, any change might easily be an improvement. Neither attitude was sane, but the boss' was at least human.

"Yeah?"

The voice of the man on the other end of the line came to Danny a little late, rebroadcast through the filtering reflexes of the intervening mind. *Boss, there's heavy cars on the road. Not cops, but some kind of raid, looks like. Maybe the Pinks.*

"If it was cops Impy would have tipped us off. Drop the shutters and get ready for 'em."

I

But boss, there's about five guys outside, and the guards—

"Drop the shutters, I said. They took the guard posts as the easiest jobs. Now let 'em learn different." He hung up. "All right, Tooey, stash him—what're you waiting for? The Pinks are here."

"Cripes!" Tooey said. He wrenched Danny around and propelled him through the door. A moment later there was a metallic *brang* all through the low building. The "shutters," Danny guessed, were armor-plate.

The corridor down which Danny was being prodded was empty and not very well lit. Danny felt the whirling electron-waves passing over the whorls of his forebrain; the sensation was no longer painful, but simply distracting, a little like the convulsive, not-unpleasant shiver of goose-flesh. Through it he could sense dimly the shapes of the objects with which he was in contact, and suspected that with practice the whirling waves would fade entirely, leaving him with a clearly-defined object-sense unfogged by undifferentiated sensations.

In a second, the roving PK field found the ends of Tooey's necktie, flipped them over the gorilla's shoulders, and strangled him with such indecent haste that his head fell straight back between his shoulder blades before his body had struck the floor.

If the Pinkertons were closing in on the building, Danny didn't want to be found here. Even if he were not shot in the fracas, he would have a hell of a job straightening out his actual status to the satisfaction of the Pinks, and since the Pinks took elaborate pains to cooperate with the police, his capture by them would result in his
130

involuntary bail-jumping becoming a matter of official record. If, on the other hand, he could get out of here within the next few hours, there was a chance—a very small chance, but a real one—that he might get back to his apartment before—

No, that was no good. It kept slipping his mind that his apartment had been the scene of a murder. Nevertheless, he had no intention of staying in the long low country house an instant longer than he had to.

There was no way out on the ground floor. The closer Danny came to the exits, the more he was buffeted by hunched shadows carting weapons to prepared stations, and the greater the chances of detection became. The fallen steel curtains at the exits themselves would no more pass Danny than they would pass the raiding Pinks; read minds and manipulate small objects Danny could, but walk through walls he could not.

He found a stairwell and climbed it. The pain was coming back, and it was not a pain he recognized; neither the whirling waves of PK nor the authentic, ringing headache of ESP, but a nauseating dislocation which made it difficult for him to see. He didn't understand it, and it was serious enough to be frightening; it made it difficult for him to put his feet down accurately on the stair treads.

On the second floor—actually only a furnished attic—tense figures were already crouching in the made-to-order machine-gun nests of dormer windows. At the far end, a section was partitioned off; through an open door Danny caught a split-second glimpse of a piece of electronic apparatus of fantastic size which was so out of place in

131

a gamblers' hideout that his mind refused to accept it; then that door too slid shut, moving smoothly sidewise like the door of an automatic elevator.

There was no way out here, either.

No way out, no way out, no way out.

"Hey you—get over here and make yourself useful."

No way out, no way out, no way out. His head throbbed like a cracked bell. For a crazed moment he wondered if the radio-active stuff Todd had been giving him were destroying his brain.

"Hey, what the hell—this guy's not—"

A lowering shape swung on him. The dim attic quivered and was snapped away, dwindling into distance and insignificance like a lemon seed squeezed between thumb and forefinger.

Then it was very gray and cold.

chapter ten

PASTORALE

For a long time, Danny lay where he was, the brambles piercing his clothes and scratching at his face and scalp as he gasped for breath. Not only his head, but his whole body hurt him horribly, and he was soaking wet all along one side. Closing one hand rewarded him with the feel of cold mud oozing between his fingers. The odor of decaying leaves was in his nostrils, and grayness and brightness flickered and flowed beneath his eyelids.

Distantly, guns chattered on the raw air.

Finally, he was conscious enough to wonder where he was. He opened his eyes and saw an overcast morning sky, fretted with branches. He sat up, his head hammering with every motion. He lay sprawled on one elbow until the cold wetness became intolerable, then got up, swaying. All around him, trees, leafless, swayed with him.

Without knowing why, he began to stumble away from the sounds of gunfighting. Behind his eyes, a multitude of voices murmured things that made no sense.

He reached out for Marla—but that only made the

133

kaleidoscopic murmuring louder and at the same time more indistinct. He knew that he could shut out the murmuring entirely if he chose, but the thought frightened him and he forgot it promptly.

The trees whispered, too. The little copse was dead, dead for the rest of the year, but it moved and talked, and there were little utterly savage thoughts moving inside dead logs and under the matting of dead leaves, hundreds of them, minute, single-mindedly murderous, like the thoughts of shell-fragments in flight. The whole world was a chiaroscuro of whispers and shadows.

He began to run. A stump tripped him at once, but he got up and made his aching muscles resume pumping. Branches lashed him, tree-trunks sprang squarely before him and knocked his breath out of his body, bark skinned his face and hands. But he ran.

The sight of the distant city helped, a little, to bring back to him some of the things he needed to know. He stood on the edge of the scrub forest, looking down the slope of the low mountain across extensive suburbs. The river beyond was nothing but a bank of mist on the horizon, above which the colorless, phantom shapes of city skyscrapers floated in the morning light. He stopped in dumb astonishment, weaving drunkenly. Behind him and to the left, the sounds of battle diminished.

I got out. There wasn't any way out, but I got out. I'm farther from the city than I was before.

And then:

It's like my dream of floating. I got out, but I don't know how—I got out all of a sudden, all at once.

He began to stagger down the slope toward the nearby

highway, which should lead him—should, only because he needed it to do so, not because it necessarily led anyplace at all—through the suburbs and back to the city. He did not wonder what his chances were of getting through the groomed, gardened Republicanism between himself and Marla: a scratched and soaked and ragged figure, with a face blotched on the temples and forehead with stiffening SS electrode compound blackened with accumulated dirt, obviously sick, probably drunk, certainly on no legitimate business. His mind was dead, drained of everything but the basic impulse to stay alive and to go where life was.

The psi faculties, ill-understood and undependable, had burned out. Danny remembered only dimly Todd's warning of quick fatigue—and nothing he had found in the books or had heard from Todd would explain why or how he had been snapped out here like a pebble from a sling, snapped from organized tension to the swamps of trance. The word *teleportation* came to him, but it was only a word. If it meant anything to him, it meant that now not only his head but his whole body was in pain.

And Todd was helpless now, trussed with his own wire in a stuffy closet, or under arrest as witness to a murder, notorious in the latter case and a liability to his University no matter how long his researches had drawn students, money and respect toward the University, perhaps smothered to death if still in the closet, and in any event all his study and unselfishness come to nothing, nothing at all. The psi powers were gone; except for this unfocus-

135

able and maddening murmur, they had evaporated into chill mist.

The nightmare, however, remained. There was no longer any refuge for Danny. Unless—

Wait. There was still the brownstone house. Sir Lewis Carter. If there was one man in the world to whom the truth, whatever it might be, would seem neither dangerous nor incredible, that man was Sir Lewis Carter. He had spent most of his life exploring areas of experience at which most scientists only, at the very best, shrugged, and had survived their laughter and pity with calmness and some aplomb.

He had a substantial reputation—not only for ordinary astronomical discovery, but for the invention of a form of relativistic math called non-invariation which was in no way less admired because neither Sir Lewis nor anybody else had yet been able to find a way of making an operational test of it; nobody thought the less of Sir Lewis or non-invariance because Sir Lewis also happened to believe in spirits, though his explorations of the marches of the psychic had been widely regretted. He had survived the gibes of the press and the rare attacks of less imaginative men in his own field with equal determination, even with equanimity and good humor.

There was, at least, a haven for Danny at the Psychic Research Society. Sir Lewis could hide him—long enough for Danny to get some rest, if no longer. After that—

After that the future was blank. Catastrophe most certainly crouched in it; but it was hidden.

Danny shuffled his uncertain way through the stubble toward the highway.

chapter eleven

THE ADEPTS

When Danny awoke he felt nearly rested, though he was still stiff all over. Late afternoon sunlight was streaming in upon him through a tiny barred window. The bars were the criss-cross kind common to the first floors of brownstone houses, though the window did not seem to be on the ground floor.

The chrome-steel grating that served for a door to Danny's room certainly was not common to brownstones, or to any other kind of building except a prison. Danny sat up on his cot and stared at it, cleaning the corners of his eyes with his fingers. But the clearer the gleaming bars became, the less sense they made.

Had he passed out on the road, and been picked up by the police, or—at last—by the FBI?

But he could clearly remember stumbling up the front steps of the Psychic Research Society's office. He could remember, as well, his dim sensation of surprise as the door opened while he was fumbling for the bell; and he had a clear picture of Sir Lewis Carter, and a clear recall of the astrophysicist's deep, friendly voice, saying, "Come in, my boy. We were just talking about you."

Some time after that he had passed out—perhaps almost immediately. He couldn't remember now. Sir Lewis and two other men, the latter in deep crimson robes like those of monks, had had some sort of conversation, and then—and then—

He couldn't remember. Still it seemed likely that he had not left the brownstone. Were the bars, then, there to keep him in—or to keep someone else out?

There was his dream of floating—had that been only the dream it seemed, or had he actually been drifting outside his apartment like some grotesque balloon? Perhaps the bars were there for his own protection while he slept. As an explanation it was anything but satisfactory, but it was the only one that occurred to him.

He became conscious once more of that indistinct, multifarious murmuring inside his skull. It both pleased and disturbed him. It meant that his developing telepathic sense had not burned out for good, and that he had probably passed the stage where telepathy, at least, would persist in cutting itself in and out of his mental circuits without any volition on his part. He was a telepath for good.

But he still could not select any one stream of consciousness out from all the pulsing "voices." He would have liked to search for Todd and Marla, but again a tentative attempt to detect them simply made the murmuring louder and more confusing. There were several million minds between Danny and the other two, all indistinguishable from one another except at very close range.

Telepathy, as Dr. Rhine had shown years ago at Duke University, was not in any way comparable with radio—people were not neatly spread out along a wave-band like broadcasting stations, each with his own allocated individual wavelength. People's brains travelled with the people who owned them, and so did the thoughts which passed through those brains, scattered helter-skelter all over the Earth in patternless and ever-changing positions.

Nor was there any analogy in telepathy for "sending" and "receiving," though parapsychologists used the terms for convenience. Telepathy was, instead, just one factor of ESP; it was a perception, not an action, and as nearly passive as the detection of a sound or feeling the impact of a blow. The telepath perceived the thought, as he would perceive any other event in space-time. The mind which held the thought did not need to "send" it, and if it were the mind of a non-telepath, it could never "receive" anything which did not come to it through the usual channels of the senses.

Nevertheless, there should be some principle by which telepathic attention could be focused on the desired thought; by which the mind to be read could be selected from all other minds. The evidence in the Rhine works had taught Danny that thought-detecting was not limited by distance. But he didn't know how to go about it.

There was a stir beyond the bars. Danny looked up. It was Sir Lewis and the bulky, anonymous men, in the robes he had remembered.

139

"Good afternoon, my boy," Sir Lewis said. "I trust you're rested."

"Rested, but puzzled, sir," Danny said. "I seem to be behind bars. Would you tell me what they're for?"

"The bars? Why, to maintain the status quo, pending a decision. That's one of the commonest of all uses for bars." Sir Lewis smiled as if that explained everything. While he was smiling, there was a loud buzzing noise, and the bars across the doorway slid aside. "Our Council is meeting now. I expect we'll know the whole story within an hour or so."

"What story?"

"What disposition we are to make of your case. I'm afraid you've become rather an embarrassment to the Brotherhood, but we'll do the best we can. You'll be able to plead your own case, of course, and if you should find yourself in a tight corner at any time during the proceedings, bear in mind that I am on your side. So is at least one other Council member, to my certain knowledge."

"Excuse me, Sir Lewis, but I don't make the slightest sense of what you're telling me. Furthermore I'm beginning to feel as if I've come to the wrong place. May I go home, please?"

"No," said Sir Lewis, quite pleasantly. "Let me see, do you have a water tumbler in here? Ah, yes. Fill it, please, and take this."

"This" was a gray pill about the size and shape of a robin's egg. Danny eyed it with disbelief.

"I'd have to be a horse to get that down. What is it?"

"It is a requirement," Sir Lewis said blandly. "Take it, please."

140

"Impossible." And not only impossible: frightening. There was something wrong with the little egg, which Danny could now see was made of metal. He wanted nothing to do with it, now or ever; he did not even want to touch it.

"You're quite sure?"

"Take it away. I'm tired of it already; I want a plush dog on wheels."

Sir Lewis moved his head slightly. The men in the deep crimson robes stepped forward with the explosive grace of panthers and locked Danny's arms to his sides.

"What the—"

Sir Lewis deftly thumbed the huge bolus into Danny's mouth, emptied the water tumbler after it, and held Danny's nose. Danny gagged and retched, but the astronomer, undiscouraged, crowded the metal egg right back in, and held Danny's mouth shut too.

For a moment Danny glared at him furiously, breathing around the egg between his teeth.

"It's no good, Mr. Caiden," the astronomer said calmly. "I can, of course, cover your mouth completely with my palm, and even though you turn as blue as a child in a tantrum, eventually you will have to swallow. Do so now and save yourself the struggle."

Danny tried to kick him, but Sir Lewis evaded his swinging shoe with a motion which seemed to be measurable only in fractions of an inch. "Also," Sir Lewis said, "I am a telepath, of course, so your chances of making any move I cannot detect the moment it occurs to you are nil. *Swallow!*"

Danny swallowed. Sir Lewis let go of him, but the two

141

men remained at his sides. It was just as well. The agony
of getting the bulky object down left him needing support.
He could feel the thing inching down his gullet; it felt as
if he had swallowed a basketball.

After a moment he also felt something else, and learned
why he had been afraid of the metal egg. The murmuring
inside his head was gone. In its place was a horrible scram-
bling dislocation, not only of the telepathic impressions,
but even of his own thoughts. He found himself incapable
of thinking a sentence through without a reeling dizziness
which threatened to black out the whole room. It was a
little like being nearly blind drunk, but even that compari-
son fell far short of the reality.

Sir Lewis watched him for a moment, then nodded. "A
resonator," he said. "It induces eddy currents from every
sensory impulse; very confusing to the mind, as you see."

"Why?" Danny gasped.

"The Brotherhood wants to take no chances, Mr. Caiden.
It would be awkward for us if you were to hypnotize someone, raise a fire, teleport yourself out of the building—
truthfully we don't know just how extensive your talents
are. But we can depend upon the little apparatus to—ah—
be with you until we reach some decision."

"What Brotherhood? What's this all about?" The effort
to frame the questions made him dizzy again. Evidently
the resonator left him only enough cortical energy to carry
on one kind of thinking at a time. If he wanted to speak,
he'd have to expect to be unable to see while talking—or
to hear, for that matter. The thing was a rape of sanity.

It bespoke also a knowledge of the psi faculties, and a
technique in handling them, beside which Danny's nascent
142

abilities could be compared only to the rudimentary thoughts of insects which he had sensed while in the forest.

"The Brotherhood," Sir Lewis was saying, "is the Brotherhood In Psi, of which I have the honor to be Hegemon. We were decidedly surprised when you blundered up our steps. At that same moment, our Council was seated in solemn session to determine whether you too should be a frater, or should instead be eliminated. Your arrival swung most of the Council against you; the majority opinion is that our deliberations led you to us despite the fact that the Council room walls are supposed to be thought-proof. The fraters think such sensitivity freakish and dangerous."

"Thought-proof?" Danny echoed. "There's no such thing, Sir Lewis."

"You haven't met some of our Councillors." The astronomer turned abruptly. "Come along, please."

Danny had no choice. The two musclemen at his sides propelled him firmly along the corridor and into a small automatic elevator. The artificial jangling in his mind continued, like a perpetual whirlwind of tambourines.

The Council members were robed and cowled like the two PRS members who had conducted Danny to the meeting. They sat immobile at a diamond-shaped table until Sir Lewis seated himself; then they turned and looked at Danny, all of them at once, their dim faces pasty in the shadows of the cowls.

"Is this the candidate?"

"Hell, no," Danny said. "If you want me, you'd damn well better ask me politely whether or not I want you."

When the blackout lifted, the nine cowled men were all

looking at Sir Lewis. "Frater Hegemon, we understood that the candidate was to be brought here under resonance," someone said.

"He is, I assure you," Sir Lewis said. "The Council will please remember that Mr. Caiden is an unusually gifted candidate—something of a polymath in our field, and potentially the superior of us all. Otherwise this meeting would have been unnecessary."

There was a stir among the delegates. They didn't like that, these men in their mumbo-jumbo robes.

"Are you certain that there is no question of psychic activity?"

"None whatsoever, Frater Histor. You may sense that for yourself. You may expect, however, that Mr. Caiden will be in better possession of his mother wit than would most of you under like circumstances. Conduct yourselves accordingly."

Another stir.

"Would you bear in mind, Frater Hegemon, that the Epiprytanis is in charge in the absence of the Prytanis? We don't have officers for nothing."

"Perhaps not," Sir Lewis said. "I mean only to warn you all, however, that the man you are judging is a dangerous man. We will all pay dearly for any stupidity we allow at this meeting. And since it's my function to maintain order, I give you all notice that I will take personal action against any frater who does not treat this candidate as if he were made entirely of nitroglycerine."

There was no answer. Sir Lewis was giving the Brotherhood rough handling. But there was still no hint of what they wanted of him, or of what they did with themselves

144

when they weren't acting like characters in an historical play.

"Let's get on with it," the man who had called himself the Epiprytanis said.

"Quite," said Sir Lewis. "Mr. Caiden."

"That's my name."

"Try to maintain an open mind," Sir Lewis said. "Your attitude toward us is hostile, and you have good reasons for your hostility. But I assure you that our precautions were not any more drastic than was absolutely necessary —and that the game is, in the end, worth the candle. Every man you see before you now is an adept in the handling of some psychic force. Some of us, like myself, are telepaths— some are hypnotists—some are teleports—some clairvoyants, some pyrotics, some telekineticists, and so on for some distance.

"It happens rarely that a man is born with one or another of these gifts. The average human being has never considered the powers that lie in the mind, or, if he has considered them, has so considered only to scoff or to prattle superstition. It takes thought to explore the psychic continuum, and most people prefer astrology to thought.

"You are here because you've taken thought on the gifts that you have and have made something of them. Your gifts are real; and on the first day that you came to the PRS to consult us, you became eligible, automatically, for membership in the Brotherhood."

"All right," Danny said. "I'm eligible. Maybe I should try to ignore your recruiting methods and 'maintain an open mind,' though how I can do that with this roc's egg in my stomach—oh, hell."

K   145

When the darkness lifted, they were still waiting for him. If anything had been said in the interim, he would never know it.

"All right. What's in it for me?"

"More than you imagine," Sir Lewis said, with great seriousness. "The rare and select human beings who can know and manipulate the psychic continuum are the hope of the race. Regardless of any democratic prejudices you may have, these people are more important to humanity than captains or statesmen or kings. This is the essence of the question, Mr. Caiden.

"But what you need to know now is that in the psychic continuum, where the mind lives and has its being, the normal laws of space-time do not apply. A man who knows this and can use the information can be—for instance—as rich as he chooses, or as powerful. This is completely incidental to the grand design, but it is real and graspable if that is what you seek."

The resonator made coherent thought almost impossible, but Danny did not need any very intricate analysis to find the bugs in Sir Lewis' "grand design."

"Men who have real power to exercise," he said, fighting to keep his maverick mind clear, "don't hide behind identical robes and synthetic mysticism. And men who have real power use it. They don't argue; they coerce."

"Of what kind of power are you speaking?" Sir Lewis asked reasonably. "We have no political power, true. That's forbidden us by the rules of our Order. One of the characteristics of the true psi-man is that he knows how little his gifts avail him in most mundane affairs. The East discovered long ago that the psychic forces are not part of the

146

space-time continuum, and are degraded by mere power-seeking."

"Are you now about to tell me that all this stuff was originally bequeathed you from some ancient Tibetan lamasery?"

"No, I'm not," Sir Lewis said, flushing under his robe. "But I assure you that it is widely known there."

"It sounds like it. As far as I'm concerned, the ancient wisdom of Tibet can be summed up in the fact that the incidence of syphilis in the population is 90%. When do we start talking sense?"

"Suppose you tell me first why you think what I say is sense-free."

Danny laughed. "Because, first of all, there is no 'psychic continuum.' Secondly, because what you call psychic 'gifts' are only side-effects of two fundamental parapsychological traits with a real existence in the physical universe. They move things in space-time, and in turn are moved. Hence they're just as useful in the pursuit of power as any other abilities, and *you're so using them*. The employment of force and fraud are the distinguishing characteristics of political power, and you're employing both."

He missed a substantial part of Sir Lewis' response in the throbbing blackness which had enveloped him the moment he had undertaken the long speech. He took advantage of the temporary divorce from his environment to think frantically while the opportunity lasted.

These people, with their talk of a "psychic continuum," obviously had no conception of the infinite series of overlapping space-time plena which, if the theory Danny and Todd had fathered on Dunne *et al.* were right, lay at the

147

roots of all the phenomena symbolized by the Greek letter
psi. This conclusion couldn't be avoided; yet the use of a
resonator to keep Danny's psi faculties out of order argued
exactly the opposite way—argued an enormous and intricate knowledge of the serial universe, and a remarkable
ability to manipulate it. Who was fooling whom? Or was
the Brotherhood comparable to Soviet science, with ritual-
istic dogma and laboratory practice kept in carefully separated pigeon-holes?

That seemed to be the best answer available. It made
the Brotherhood In Psi look more mightily unattractive
than ever. Those pigeon-holes had fluid walls, and the
dogma had a nasty way of interpenetrating the practice,
usually to the discomfort or even to the extinction of the
practitioner.

"—without notice," Sir Lewis was saying as the light
gradually came back. "Unfortunately, we're unable to
take such a view of the matter. We can't allow any man,
whatever the strength of his disagreement with us, to remain outside the Brotherhood once he has discovered that
the Brotherhood exists. Frankly I expected that you would
join us; otherwise you would still be as ignorant as ever of
the Brotherhood's existence—at least until your abilities
reached the point where you could detect it by yourself.

"So I ask you to bear in mind, Mr. Caiden, that your
agreement is needed for your own self-preservation. Naturally, we won't accept any agreement based upon that
argument and that one alone; it would be untrustworthy.
That's why I'm at such pains to bring home to you the
justice of our stand."

Danny struggled to keep his quivering, fragmented

thoughts upon the point at issue. "I won't play," he said. "I don't hold with this theory of the selectness of the psi-man. The psi faculties are latent in every man's mind. If you're all the specialists you pretend to be—and if you're really concerned with preserving the psi powers for the sake of the race—then you ought to be spreading your knowledge around, not hiding it."

"Not everyone can assimilate such knowledge," Sir Lewis said. "Not everyone has the, chromosomes for it."

"That's true in the limited sense that not everyone has two eyes and five fingers. There is such a thing as heredi-tary blindness, and there is such a thing as syndactyly. Both are very rare. Your society is founded on the principle that a man with two eyes and five fingers is somehow superior to a man who hasn't yet bothered to count how many he's got.

"Actually your noble pretensions are blatherskite. You're keeping your powers a secret because they give you enor-mous advantages over people who are ignorant of them. There could be no other reason and there doesn't need to be any other. You've set up a master-race theory to justify yourselves to yourselves because each of you has some one limited psi faculty—but *all* the psi faculties are avail-able to *everyone*, with good training. I'm the living proof of that; no more ordinary guy ever walked the Earth until I was given skilled help. Now I'm so good at this stuff I've got you all wetting your pants, and I'm still developing. You call yourselves experts, but you can't even tell the psi faculties apart from non-parapsychological functions—hell, you still think hypnotism is a psi faculty! A cheap stage magician knows better than that."

149

He wished fervently that he could have seen the reactions of the cowled figures, but the roaring darkness engulfed him and would not go away. Of one thing he was sure: he had just talked himself into a coffin, barring a new miracle.

Somehow, he didn't care. He had seen several miracles recently; and the pleasure of getting in a few licks of his own had been intensely rewarding after so many days and nights of being harried without letup. He understood, now, why small children, once goaded to defiance, become even more defiant in the face of certain punishment.

When his sight finally began to clear, the Brotherhood was motionless and silent.

Finally, Sir Lewis said, "Are there questions from the board?"

No one said anything.

"I call for a vote," the man called the Epiprytanis said.

One by one, the cowled figures rose and left the room. At length there was only Sir Lewis and another man and Danny.

"I vote to retain the candidate," the unknown man said. "His kind of thinking is rare and valuable. In my opinion it's time we outgrew playing fancy dress and put our attentions to a good, thorough, naked power-grab—at which game Mr. Caiden could be invaluable to us. He knows things that we don't, obviously. We need him."

Sir Lewis spread his hands. "You saw how the vote went."

"Set it aside."

"Impossible."

The unknown man said: "Then the Brotherhood is out-
150

moded. The others were right all the time. I'm leaving, Sir Lewis."

But instead of leaving, the dissenter sprang up from the table with an unbearable shriek, tearing at his robe. A thick pillar of greasy smoke began to rise straight up from him. He screamed again—and then he was a shadow inside a long blade of white flame.

The flame gave no heat and nothing outside it was burned. It lasted perhaps four seconds, and vanished. Shrivelled and carbon black, a thing like a mummy of a dwarf toppled upon the carpet.

Sick, Danny said: "You had a pyrotic on him."

"Yes," Sir Lewis said. "We use only psychic weapons— another of our rules which strike you as so foolish."

"Not at all. You'll teleport the body to his bed at his home, and the Forteans will have themselves another case history as soon as the cops discover it. No traces, no explanation—hence, no investigation possible. A smart rule."

When he could see again, the body was gone, and Sir Lewis was watching him.

"I'm sorry, Danny. I like you, and I did my best."

"Skip it. When do I get the heat-treatment?"

Sir Lewis shrugged. "As soon as my ability to postpone it is outweighed by the impatience of the others. They fear you, I'm afraid. Especially our Prytanis fears you; he refused even to be present at the meeting, though he's attended every other one for decades. And Danny, you didn't go out of your way to cooperate with us."

There was a long silence. At last Sir Lewis said, "Do you know the man who was burned?"

"No," Danny said. "And he didn't sound to me like

someone I would want to know. You've got a nice nestful of bad eggs here." He fought away the black dizziness. "What about you? You've been painting yourself as a friend, or at least as an advocate."

"I? I'm bound by the rules of the Order. I surrendered my personal preferences long ago. I'll postpone your execution as long as I can, as I've said, in the hope that something will happen to reverse the decision. But when the time runs out, that will end the matter. The preservation of the Order means more to me than your life, simply because, Danny, it means more to me than my own."

Danny said: "We, who are about to die, salute you—you egghead."

chapter twelve

THUNDERBOLT

The room was a fairly comfortably spot—as cells go. It was roughly twelve feet square, and since it was on the corner of the building, it had two windows. Neither one of them was large enough to pass a man, even had it been unbarred.

The barred door was of the electrically-controlled sliding type used in modern prisons. It was open or shut by a switch in some central office, so there were no keys to be snatched from careless guards. Furthermore, shorting it would not provide a freedom longer than a moment at most, since—as Danny had noticed when it had opened for Sir Lewis—it was provided with an extremely noisy buzzer which began to sound as soon as electrical contact between lock and doorframe was broken, and which could be depended upon to have a separate power source.

Still, the cell wasn't bad. It was clean and dry, and the north window looked down upon the heavy traffic of a produce market district, where huge trailer trucks unloaded fresh fruits and vegetables all night long in the glare of mercury vapor lamps, and smaller trucks and delivery wagons hauled it away to warehouses and grocery stores during the day through clouds of exhaust fumes. Not, perhaps, a restful environment, but an interesting one for an ex-food-editor.

The window on the other wall was tiny, and seemed to overlook nothing but a sort of vertical channel or groove in the building's wall. On the back face of the channel was another window, boarded up and bound with still another board nailed laterally. On the lateral board were stencilled white letters, much washed out, which Danny finally managed to read by a combination of squinting and imagination; they said: *Shaftway*.

As for the inside of the cell, the cot was surprisingly comfortable; the plumbing arrangements were modern, though decidedly public; the sink had one spring cold-water tap, and on it was the unpleasantly familiar plastic water tumbler and a cake of yellow laundry soap; the floors, walls and ceiling were faced with firebrick—and that was that.

Danny inspected everything minutely, but found nothing to encourage him. He was willing to lay odds that an experienced graduate of Alcatraz couldn't have found a way out—especially since he seemed to be the only prisoner in the place, and this the only cell. After the inspection, he began to pace, leaving his cot drawn up on its latch against the wall. He could not help the pacing; only a sheep would sit and wait to be slaughtered, and the continuous jangling in his mind helped to keep him moving as aimlessly as a penned bull in heat.

When the analogy hit him he forced himself to stop

154

stalking, to go over to the wall and let the cot down again, to sit quietly. Walking was no substitute for thinking; and, whatever the physical distraction, no matter how urgent and impossible to cope with, he had to think. If it allowed only partial thinking, then he would have to think in fragments; but he would have to think.

Yet he had to begin thinking by wishing desperately that he were rid of the resonator. As he remembered the normal rhythm of the digestive process, he couldn't expect to say goodbye to the infernal nugget for another thirty-eight hours. It was probably still in his stomach at the moment. He would simply have to work out some system for getting along with it, a prospect which he did not take to be quite so hopeless as he would have thought when he had been first forced to swallow the machine; he had been able to shorten the blackout periods and lengthen the chains of thought it would allow him even during the course of the Council meeting, first by ignoring the muddling-up of his new and still not very personalized psi faculties, second by so pacing his cortical thought-chains that no single thought was elaborate enough to penalize him with a long interruption. The subliminal flickerings of associations and memories on which coherent, formal thought depended had been unaffected by the resonator from the beginning; it seemed to have been designed only to prevent psi activity and to prevent reasoning of a comparitively high order. He could do nothing about the psi interference, but he could already reason around the device with fair facility.

In the still-shimmering chaos inside his skull all these ideas did not at first add up to anything more than the

155

promise that he would be able to think at least as well as a food editor even while the resonator was in his guts. When the long-delayed and distorted idea formed, however, he found himself trembling with excitement.

He had the resonator. It was an intimate and personal possession, and a powerful tool if he could gain access to it. If the comparatively tiny thing functioned in principle as Todd's resonator had, it would be setting up a continuous shuttling of nervous impulses between three or four "frames" or Poisson-brackets of the serial universe—the frame he would normally occupy in space-time, the frame in his immediate past, and one in the immediate future. No other operation could cause the mental eddy-currents which Sir Lewis had said the resonator created in the brain of its victim.

It was, in short, an amplifier—an amplifier for the psi faculties. It was tuned now to spread and confuse those faculties; to cause a continuous shuttling between frames, like alternating current, in order to block precise psychic orientation. But unless it was a highly simplified, one-purpose device, it could be adjusted.

And Danny had it safely in his stomach.

He strode over to the washstand, picked up the bar of yellow soap, and systematically began to eat it.

Despite his brief sleep, he was still tense with basic exhaustion, and he had had nothing to eat for quite a while. The alkaline, naphthalated stearates began to back up on him almost at once.

It was painful—the thing he wanted back was large—but he held the spring faucet open and kept at it. In half an hour, dizzy with triumph and nausea, he had the metal egg in his hand. He washed it and looked it over.

The two halves of the casing were lightly soldered together over a tight fitting; evidently the resonator had been designed to be opened for repairs, but had never been so opened by anyone in the Brotherhood. Danny grinned tightly. Dogma: a thing completed is a thing perfect. They were running true to form; they had assigned their machine its one purpose, and had closed it, to their minds, forever, though the technician who had made it for them and given it its light solder seal had known better.

The Brotherhood had relieved him of his jackknife, but they had left him something far more useful: a tiny electrician's screwdriver, part of the kit Todd had brought with him so long ago, which now hung in Danny's shirt pocket, its amber handle suspended on a fountain-pen clip. With the flap of the old Army shirt buttoned down over it, the pocket had looked empty.

That had been the Brotherhood's second slip. Leaving him soap had been the first, and the most important; he could have gotten along without the screwdriver, but it made things easy to have the screwdriver along. Without it he would have used his thumbnail; but without the soap he would still have been helpless.

He cleaned away the solder, which was quite soft and only lightly tinned to the metal, and pried one half of the casing off. The little mechanism inside was a marvel of designing. It contained only one tube, a thing about the size of a peppercorn, and most of its circuits were printed in the inner surfaces of a sheet of laminated lucite. Todd's series of steps had been summed up in a single trans-

157

former, into the minute casing of which were set two wristwatched-sized set-screws. Probably the final stages of assembly had been carried on under a binocular microscope.

Most of the innards were hidden, but Danny knew better than to expect to understand the device at a glance. All he needed to know now was embodied in those two set-screws.

The resonator was adjustable.

He filed the blade of the screwdriver on the stone windowsill until it was thin enough at the point to fit the set-screw slots. Then he cautiously turned the first one.

Peace settled over him like a warm cloud. The uncontrollable jittering of his cortical impulses had stopped.

After a moment he noticed that the telepathic murmuring was gone, too. That was no good; he was going to need every psi power he could muster. He turned the screw a little further.

The jangling confusion came back. Hastily he returned the screw to its previous position.

The resonator evidently could "spread" the nervous impulses in either time direction, probably a good deal farther than the unaided mind could drive them; or it could confine them rigidly to a single frame, the normal situation of the mind without psi powers. The latter situation meant no bleeding away of volitional control, but it meant no possibility of using the psi faculties, either. They depended upon complete, open contact with the alternate frames of the serial universe.

If he was to have any chance whatsoever of getting out of here, before the Brotherhood put one of its pyrotics on him or stuffed him down some manhole, he'd have to figure out how to get the psychic spread back without sacrificing the cortical control. He considered simply setting the resonator at neutral and throwing it away, depending thereafter upon his natural psychic abilities, but, entirely aside from the risk involved, that was out of the question: at worst the device would be invaluable to Todd, and at best, properly understood, it could be made to work for Danny.

There were two set-screws. Mathematically, each one should represent a variable in that basic psi equation Todd had been trying to find. The PK equation had turned out to be the already well-known Blackett-Dirac formula; the ESP equation had also worked out to something quite familiar and standard to Todd, although new to Danny. Todd had then been seeking the master equation of which the two were either functions or derivatives—probably, he had said, the former. He had tackled it as a problem in matrix calculus, involving Heisenberg's "probability packets," and had nearly had it licked when the mobsters had intervened.

Now Danny, who had no mathematical ability whatsoever, and less knowledge of the field, had to try to find it for himself. He had nothing to go on but the possibility that the master equation was also something quite familiar and well-known; plus the fact that in the course of his frantic researches he had run across quite a few such equations—particularly in the appendices of Count Korzybski's *Science and Sanity*.

He rummaged in the incredible lumber-room of fact, distortion, fantasy and lie which his reading—or rather, his

ESP memorizing—had dumped at random into his head, trying to locate the original Heisenberg "indeterminacy" formulation. There it was, together with several pages of text and footnotes on what it was all about. It ran:

$$pq-qp = h/2 \; ii \; ^1 \; (1)$$

The (1), however, did not turn out to be part of it; that just made it "Equation No. 1" in Korzybski's exposition. Danny scanned the visualized pages. The q was the generalized coordinate; insofar as Danny could follow Korzybski's discussion of it, it didn't bear on his present problem. The p was momentum, and h was the Planck constant, which was a quantity imported into the equation from thermodynamics, a science about which he knew even less than he knew about math. It began to look hopeless, as he knew he should have suspected from the beginning. If it had taken Todd all night to get to first base—

But Todd was a scientist and would not jump to conclusions until all the evidence was in, even had he possessed the major clue which was the resonator. Danny was being forced to jump, and jump fast. Momentum, at least, he understood; in terms of the psi powers it would probably be equal to the velocity of propagation of nerve impulses, which was, as nearly as Danny could remember, in the neighborhood of 60 feet per second. Change that velocity, and you change the amplification of the machine that ran on it, the brain, and hence the brain's range of detection. That accounted for the first set-screw—but he already knew, in the practical sense, how that one worked.

There seemed to be nothing in the equation to account for the other one. Planck's constant was a constant, and that was that; besides, it was an impossibly tiny sum—

6.547 x 10—^{27} erg-seconds, according to the visualized text; it would be indetectable except in the realm of the electron. It was a quantum-value—

Which would vary in an infinitely overlapping series.

There it was, staring him in the face. Necessarily, h would change in value at a constant rate from frame to frame; it was, in fact, the difference which kept the frames separated from each other.

The timing principle!

Somebody in the PRS-Brotherhood had gotten his head up out of the mush of the "psychic continuum," that was evident. With shaking fingers, Danny inserted the screwdriver into the slot of the second screw and turned it a fraction of a degree; then he opened the second screw wide.

The first thing he heard was a single word, in a perfectly clear and recognizable mental voice. The word was:

"Attaboy!"

The voice was—Sean Hennessy's.

The second thing that Danny heard was a long muttered grumbling, deeper than the rumble of the produce trucks. Capping the resonator carefully, he stepped to the north window.

The fraction of the night sky which was visible was covered with low-scudding, boiling clouds. While he watched, sheet-lightning obliterated them; then they came back, the neon-tinted glare of the city painting their undersides. A storm was coming up. Danny counted the seconds from the flash until the roll of thunder reached him: One-and-a-one, two-and-a-two, three-and-a-three, four-and-a-four, five-and-a-five . . . At thirty he heard it; less than eight miles away, then, and coming on fast.

He changed his plans on the instant. It should be possible, now that the resonator was available to help, instead of lodged in him like a cancer, for him to teleport himself out of the building, as he had unintentionally teleported himself out of the gambling syndicate's hideout; but he had a hunch that it wouldn't be wise—and these days he trusted his hunches. Simply skipping would not solve anything now. There were too many unknowns, and too many threads which had to be held against unravelling. He would have to locate Marla and Todd, and probably bail them out of what must now have accumulated into a wild confusion of trouble; he would have to get himself clear of the net of circumstantial evidence the FBI had flung about him, and of the violation of bond of which he was already, however inadvertently, registered as guilty; and above all, he would have to vanish from the ken of the Brotherhood and stay vanished, without any use of psi powers extensive enough to enable them to pinpoint him or even to suspect that he was still alive. To elude the PRS, he would have to contrive a convincing substitute for death.

The thunder rumbled again as Danny left the window. The PRS was still to some extent an unknown quantity, but it was a cinch that it was a nest of trouble, and of a highly sensitive kind of trouble which could come smelling after him like a hunting cheetah. Remembering his first visit to the brownstone, Danny grinned ruefully. He'd stuck his head right into the proverbial lion's mouth, and the lion had just yawned—but its eyes had been open.

162

Danny could sense the men of the Brotherhood now, moving through the building, intent upon their still-unknown affairs. One of those men was bound to be a clairvoyant, mentally posted to Danny's cell—an adept who would give the alarm at once if that cell should suddenly become untenanted. Then would come a concentrated sweep of all the surrounding area, using every psi ability available to the Brotherhood; and then a pyrotic, homed on Danny by telepaths and PK sensitives, would be called in to raise around him, wherever he was, a cocoon of flame which would consume nothing but himself . . .

He could not leave the cell without covering his tracks.

A sudden flash of lightning cast criss-cross patterns on the floor through the window. Despite himself, Danny jumped. The burst of electrical light had seemed entirely too close for comfort. Three seconds later came a battery of thunder, wild and deafening.

The storm was about to break.

If the place could be struck by lightning, for instance—

Well—why not? The earth-sky relationship which made for lightning had been known for two hundred years; it was a simple problem in static electricity. Even books on the grammar-school level described the widening of potential-difference between cloud and ground, the preparatory upstroke, the bolt which put the two charges back into temporary balance. If a man could use PK to throw around as complicated an assemblage of unit charges as a piece of furniture, why couldn't he move free positrons in large enough quantity to attract the greedy masses of electrons in a thunderhead?

A premonitory, undisciplined surge of particles, spread-

163

ing eagerly across his frontal lobes, told him that it could be done.

But it had to be done quickly; the storm was passing overhead and away with every second, and the Brotherhood's will that he should die was closing upon him at least as rapidly.

Opening the resonator again, he stationed himself in the southwest corner of the cell, and turned both setscrews as far as they would go—in effect turning the gain all the way up, and the tuner to "local." Then he focussed every erg of his enormously boosted psi energy upon the opposite corner. Deliberately putting out of his mind every thought of Marla, of Todd, of the PRS, of himself, he concentrated upon driving every free electron out of that corner of the building.

There was plenty of resistance. The space-lattice of atomic nuclei in the stone was not as regular as it would have been in metal, so that the wandering charges tended to gravitate toward the nearest source of binding energy and become planetary; essentially, Danny was trying to make a substance which was a nearly perfect insulator conduct electricity. It was easy enough to chase away the surface charge, which was the main mass-charge anyhow, but the buried charge stubbornly fought back. By driving the free positrons inward at the same time, however, he slowly tipped the balance . . .

Footsteps sounded hollowly in the corridor, and in the back of his mind he felt a pressure, as if an enormously heavy stone were being lowered upon him. He did not know what it was and did not want to wait to find out. There were only a few seconds left—was the charge high

164

enough? There was also the alternate danger—if it were too high, he would surely be electrocuted. Stone was a poor conductor, and he'd have to chance any nimbus effect. He tightened his grip on the re-capped resonator, and hurried and harried the fleeing electrons.

Someone stopped outside the bars and peered in.

Now!

With a last, an ultimate mental thrust, he drove open a channel for the bunched positrons, sending them fountaining invisibly skyward. A blinding forest of lightning bolts leapt into being outside the window. The thunderclap that came with it was worse than anything he had ever heard on a battlefield; it fell on him like a lead door. The whole universe burst into flame and toppled into final darkness in a blast of noise.

With it toppled Danny, every muscle knotted with galvanic tetanus—blind, deaf, stunned, convulsed, helpless.

chapter thirteen

THE KING OF EAGLES

The bubble that was space-time expanded into infinity; the stars blackened and died; the entropy gradient ran down, and there was an end of motion. The universe had died its ultimate, inevitable heat-death. Fifty billion years.

Then it began to collapse inward upon itself. The evenly distributed molecules of cold gas closed in upon one another. Suddenly space-time seethed with stripped atoms, and then with the primordial flux of neutrons, the ylem; then the whole enormous mass had contracted into a single mathematical point, the primordial atom. Fifty billion years.

Creation began.

In the glaring white, whirling uniformity it was impossible to tell just when the Earth was born; but it was already three billion years old when the agonizing stiffness began to abate in Danny's contorted body. An even more painful prickling ran through his arms and legs, as if his muscles had been "asleep," and the blood were now returning to the surface channels.

The roar and flash of the lightning-play penetrated gradually to him, then began to diminish a little. He stirred.
The movement forced a low groan from someone he was
just beginning to think of as himself. Something dug
sharply into his back.

His toes were prickling now. He tried opening his eyes,
and was surprised to find that he could see through them,
although what he saw was impossible to understand: a
flickering blackness, and gray surfaces and dark lines re-
ceding into it.

Experimentally, he tried to sit up. A spasm of pain shot
through his hips and back. After a while, however, he
managed to force himself up on one elbow.

He seemed to be lying on a sharply sloping hill of brick,
plaster, and other rubble. Twenty feet above him, a toilet
jutted out of the shattered side of a building, bent double
on its piping like an obscene lily, fountaining a spray of
sterile nectar down over the tumbled ruins. A cloud of
brick-dust was still rising, and in the sky overhead the
clouds bashed their ram's-heads together noisily.

At the bottom of the hill, a truck trailer was lying on its
side, its tractor free of the rubble but tilted precariously,
motor still running. The collapsed side of the brownstone
had nearly engulfed it.

Danny realized suddenly that his right hand was shaking with fatigue, as violently as if he had been hanging by
it for hours. Curiously he opened it.

The resonator lay in his palm.

He managed to grin. If he had not known before what
a death-grip was, he knew now. He put the tiny, invalua-

167

ble mechanism carefully in his shirt pocket and buttoned the flap.

Then he clambered painfully to his feet and picked his way, gingerly, backwards, down the shifting uncertain hillside to the upturned side of the trailer, eased himself over the edge of the roof, and dropped to the littered ground, half-sliding against the curved, fluted metal. He fell when he hit, but was able to pick himself up again almost at once and walk shakily to the tractor.

It would do. He clambered up onto the tilted fender and worked the door open. Inside the cab, lying under the wheel on the down side, there was a body, rigid with the instantaneous stiffness of electrocution. The smell of burned flesh, sickeningly like that of roast glazed ham, mingled incongrously with a strong odor of fresh celery welling from the fallen trailer.

Danny heaved the body over to the door, handling the plushy, baked shoulders of the dead driver with a deliberate and stony ignorance of what he was touching, and tumbled it out. He slammed the cab door and settled himself on the tipped cushion before the wheel. The motor continued to run, with tiger-purrs.

Something was burning in the produce market; people were shouting. Time to go. After a brief search along the dash, Danny found the air valve, which held the trailer sealed to the truck. He opened it. The cab settled back to an even keel with a sodden sigh.

"Cascelli? Cascelli! Get the hell out of that cab, Trewater's place is on fire, give us a hand—"

Danny stepped on the gas. The drive-wheels chewed into the asphalt and carried the truck away. Behind him,

168

Danny heard a roar of collapsing masonry, as the trailer tipped over one remaining inch and was buried. Then the sound was swallowed in thunder.

And now what?

He had managed to get the universe born and bring it up to date, though he was sure he wouldn't be willing to go through it again. He was out of the PRS. He had a truck, a means of transportation to a haven unknown. At the moment he was fairly safe from the police; and as for the FBI, they couldn't be everyplace at once. They even occasionally lost Communists.

But there was now no refuge at all.

His apartment was out—that would be watched, maybe occupied. Probably the old job at Delta Publishing would be watched, too. The PRS embodied a goal, in a distorted and vicious form, but it had declared itself his enemy. Neither the Forteans nor the parapsychology center were far enough advanced into the realms of supranormality to be asked to risk offering shelter to a bail-jumper.

He was also, he realized suddenly, a murderer and an arsonist; or was he entitled to think of the running psychic battle as a form of warfare? The thought passed, leaving him basically undisturbed. His own life had been at stake, and he had struck back with as much precision as the circumstances allowed; that settled the matter.

For the moment, at any event, he was a free agent. He was just one more truck driver, prowling the traffic-heavy streets of a storm-ridden city. Sir Lewis no longer knew where he was, and might even think him dead. Neither did the FBI. Since there was no telephone in the cab, he was even out of Sean's range.

169

The traffic light ahead flickered, and Danny swung his monoxide-breathing mastodon down a side street. There'd be no sense in attracting the attention of cops by careless driving. If he obeyed the traffic signals and kept out of scrapes, he'd be just one more truck on the way to pick up a trailer. In the meantime—

In the meantime, it was going to have to be Sean. Clearly Sean had meant to be overheard when he had offered his one-word congratulation to Danny for working out the puzzle of the resonator. And equally clearly he was involved in this business somewhere, despite his very vocal skepticism.

Danny ran over his memory of that one word, listening especially to its quality, its "sound." It had a peculiarly remote, eerie quality to it, quite unlike the overheard thoughts of Tooey and the boss racketeer, almost as if it had come along some special channel reserved for extraordinary communications—he had almost thought "official." But since there were no channels in telepathy, Sean must have imparted that coloration to the word deliberately— a code, an identification tag—

If Danny could place that coloring, he could read the code. The quality of the word had one feature which was unlike normal thought; it sounded—

Underground.

Sean had been one of the voices Danny had heard on the first night. The one that had said, *"Let the finder beware."*

The psychiatric advice, the involved statistical arguments, all that had been a blind—but a blind for what?

Was everyone in this game carrying all his cards up his sleeve? It was time to find out.

It was a cinch, at least, that Sean wouldn't care a snap of the fingers whether or not the FBI was interested in Danny. Very probably, the idea would excite him; when Nietzsche had said, "Live dangerously," he was talking to Sean Hennessy.

Sean's place was a good distance away, up on 125th Street near the University. Danny turned his behemoth toward the West Side, where he could pick up a thruway to the north side of town.

Halfway there, he discovered that he was hungry. He couldn't remember having eaten anything since the liver-wurst-on-rye sandwiches, unless he counted the resonator or the soap.

He turned the truck off the thruway again and found a one-arm joint. Inside, he ordered hash-and-eggs, checked belatedly to make sure the PRS hadn't robbed him to boot, and filched a tabloid from a drunk asleep in the booth behind him. On page three there was a headline:

SNATCH WITNESS IN
PRICE-FIX PROBE
Mystery Girl Held By FBI;
Missing Scientist Is
Linked To Dead Gypsy

The story was incredibly garbled—but a few facts could be worried out of it. Todd had vanished before the cops, attracted by the shot, had arrived. Marla, evidently without stopping to think, had told the police enough about the

171

kidnapping to make them discount her story entirely; the paper had her billed as a temptress interjected into the picture by International Wheat. What Danny could not understand was how the gamblers, who evidently had survived their battle with the Pinkerton men, had managed to come back and get Todd before the cops had arrived; but on that question the story fell into total confusion.

The old man couldn't take very much rough treatment. Danny could only hope that he would tell the exact truth. The fact that both men talked the same kind of "double-talk" might puzzle the top man of the syndicate enough to make him hold off on the brutality for a while.

Marla was in no better position. She was in the cooler, where the PRS could locate her at its leisure, as soon as it had penetrated behind the scenes enough to connect her intimately with Danny. Up to now, they had never heard of her, but this kind of publicity would be more than enough to arouse their interest. If Sir Lewis hadn't been killed in the lightning barrage, he would be sure to check every possible angle; he would be far too shrewd to take Danny's "death" on faith.

Suddenly Danny was struck anew with a sense of terrible urgency. He gulped his coffee and threw a dollar bill on the table. There was nothing for it now but to get to Sean's as fast as possible, and there plan some way to get to Marla and Todd before the next storm broke.

He put the truck into gear and nosed it out onto the highway again. It was a tough assignment for an ex-trade journalist, whose only present prospect was that of hiding in a friend's apartment until the cops caught up with him, and whose only talent was faltering verse.

What kind of an assignment it might be for a man with a fully operative psi center might be another matter.

The truck's engine pounded. Danny, unused to the sound of any engine but that of a private car, wondered if it had burned out a bearing—but it ran, and it had been making that noise ever since he had put it under way. After a while, the highway turned off toward the river and ran through a quiet, dim, deserted park. Here the road split up so many times and ran in such irregular arcs that Danny almost immediately became lost. The fact that about 40% of the street lamps had been broken by stone-throwing dead-end kids made an equivalent number of road signs impossible to see. Eventually the truck emerged from the park going back the way it had come from, along a one-way street which ran on for ten blocks before allowing Danny another entrance into the park.

On the second pass he managed to emerge from the north end of the park travelling in the right direction, to find that the street numbers had already hit the hundreds. For a wonder, Sean's street, when he got to it, turned out to be one way east, which was the way he had to go. Up here the buildings consisted of nothing but enormous and expensive apartment houses, and Danny had a strong hunch that he was off limits with his noisy monster; but there was nothing he could do about it.

And there, at last, was Sean's number. With a sigh, Danny pulled the truck over to the side of the street where parking was legal for an hour and killed the engine. After

173

the hour or so he had spent in the cab, the sudden silence was vaguely alarming.

Sean was wearing a coffee-colored robe and red slippers so fuzzy that his feet appeared to have been stolen from some outrageously dyed lioness. If joblessness bothered him he did not show it. He looked perfectly composed and, as usual, faintly amused.

"Why, hello, Danny," he said. "Were *you* the cause of that racket in the street? You must have come here in a forty-ton Christie tank."

"Practically," Danny agreed. "Look, Sean. I'm in a worse jam than ever. Can you take me in? I should warn you that the FBI is after me and you'll be in trouble too if I'm found here."

"Don't talk so fast, old man, you're out of breath already," Sean said. "Yes, of course, come in. I've always wanted to be an embattled fugitive, and barring that I can always shelter one."

Gratefully, Danny went inside and dropped into a deep, low chair. The apartment was surprisingly luxurious, even for this neighborhood, where it probably rented for two hundred a month at a minimum. Sean caught Danny's wondering glance.

"Yes, it's a bit dear for an ex-food editor," he said. "But now that I'm out of that job I needn't look like a food editor any more."

"Oh. You've had dough all along and were just passing yourself off as a working man?"

"Yes, something like that. So you can see that it didn't take much courage for me to quit when you did; I felt a little guilty about taking the credit." Sean smiled gently
174

and sat down on an ottoman, stretching out one outland-ish scarlet slipper. "The time was coming when my real job would require all of my time anyhow."

"And what's that?"

"Don't you think *you* owe *me* a confidence or two, first?"

Danny felt himself flushing. It was a perfectly fair re-quest; and now that he had—so to speak—thrown himself on Sean's mercy, he didn't feel morally free to refuse.

"I figured you knew I hadn't told the whole story," he said dully. "This is it."

He talked for nearly two hours in the soft unvarying lamplight. Throughout the recital, neither Sean's expres-sion nor his position on the ottoman changed by so much as a wink. He seemed frozen in stone, one arm thrown across his lap, one leg stretched out, one hand propping up his chin. The position reminded Danny of a Doré draw-ing of Satan, and Sean's always rather diabolical hand-someness completed the impression.

It also occurred to him that such complete and unnatural physical immobility was cultivated in Yoga, where it be-spoke mental activity in inverse proportion to the degree of bodily stillness.

"I see," Sean said at last. "Fairly and truly told, and no little sacksful of reservations hidden in the mental cellar any more. Thank you, Danny."

"You're welcome, of course, Sean. You can see why I didn't want to trot all this stuff out when we first talked. Of course a lot of it hadn't happened then."

"Yes," Sean said. "Still, much of it needn't have happened at all, if you had told me everything you knew in the first place."

He stood up, hands thrust deeply into the pockets of the robe. "You see, Danny," he said, "it was quite impossible for me to be honest with you until you were honest with me. Until you told me of your own free will just how things were with you, I couldn't help you; and there were some tests I was forced to apply, also, which were unavoidably time consuming. May I see the resonator, please?"

Silently Danny passed it over. Expertly Sean sprang the shell with a pressure at its sides and inspected the interior.

"It is the same. The field feels queer, though—not right for the way you have it set. How have you been adjusting it?"

Danny showed him the screwdriver; Sean shook his head. "That's no good; you have to use a non-magnetic screwdriver, preferably a non-metallic one. Come back in the shop with me and we'll hitch it to the CRT; I don't like the idea of this distorted a field being broadcast all over creation. It's as telltale as a siren."

The "shop" evidently had been intended as a spare bedroom, but Sean had it fitted out as an electronics laboratory, the most extensive one in Danny's limited experience. Most of the equipment he could not even recognize; the cathode ray oscilloscope to which Sean was connecting the resonator was familiar, however, for Todd had had one in the University laboratory. After a few moments, luminous, contorted green traces appeared upon its television-like tube face.

176

Sean whistled. "Look at that—it's almost discontinuous," he said. "That's only partly the fault of your screwdriver; all that juice from the lightning must have knocked it further askew. If it had been behaving like this while you were in the cell, you'd never have gotten out at all."

He bent over it. The contorted wave shapes on the screen moved solemnly through new forms, like an electronic version of a Calder mobile. At last Sean was satisfied.

"There; that's the way it's supposed to go. I'll give you my sewing machine screwdriver—it's non-magnetic." He grinned at Danny. "Don't look so incredulous. I'm a bachelor too, you know; I cook, sew, make beds and keep my own checkbook straight."

He covered the resonator and handed it back to Danny. "Take care of it; it's a sensitive little gadget. I'm quite proud of it."

"*You* designed it?"

"Yes, of course—those mutton-heads at the PRS are too muzzy with mysticism to master a technique as basic as serial resonance." Sean led the way back into the living room. "I admit that I was worried as to what use they would make of it. Taylor and I estanned—"

"Taylor? The Fortean? Don't tell he's—"

"Yes. We estanned that it would probably be used on you, and that the chances were good that you'd use it to get away from the PRS. Without it, your chances looked slim—but there is always an element of uncertainty in precognition, and we couldn't be sure whether or not we were giving the PRS something with which they could do irreparable harm. But now it appears that we needn't

M   177 have worried; they used it only for what we told them it was good for, and it never even occurred to them that it might be adjustable. They're inherently incapable of scientific thinking—every time I think of that load of lab junk they've collected over the river it gets funnier."

"Who," Danny said, "is *we?* I've told my story. You tell me yours."

"Gladly," Sean said. "Real psi-men—not those ceremonious criminals at the PRS—are loosely organized all over the world. Our main purpose is research; there's a lot we don't understand yet about the serial universe, I assure you. Secondarily, we keep a close eye on people like the PRS members, people who develop some small segment or another of the parapsychological spectrum and put it to bad uses.

"The PRS, for instance, has been playing the market; they were the ones who rigged Wheat into its present position—the company itself is innocent, for a wonder— and it was their manipulations which gave your mind the first big jolt toward developing its psi powers, though they're unaware of that. They also, control, absolutely, the gambling syndicate you tangled with, and a number of other rackets. They also own most of Consolidated Warfare Service, the big Zurich munitions outfit, and a lot of lost tempers at diplomatic meetings are traceable to them. They've evolved their elaborate ritual for protecting themselves because they dread any rivalry in the field."

"Do they know of your group?"

"Yes, and they fear it; but they follow a hands-off
178

policy with us, partly from fear and partly because we represent no threat to their operations most of the time. We intervene only when it's necessary to save lives, which they know as well as we do. Their adepts can detect the development of psi powers in any individual, and, if possible, they run that individual down and enlist him—or, in the rare case where the new man has scruples, they kill him.

"Much of the time we've been able to prevent these killings, but we have a firm law against interfering until such an individual has won his way to full psi power under his own steam. If he still needs help after that—and ordinarily he doesn't—we help him. But not before."

"That's a hard rule, Sean. It's the helpless victims that need the aid more."

Sean nodded. "That's perfectly true. One of the reasons they don't get it from us, most of the time, is that we haven't the manpower to be watchdogging the PRS day and night, and when we do muscle in, we usually need the help of the victim. If he's unequipped to give it, our hands are tied; so we have had to be tough-minded about it and give up going after such people at all. In addition, believe it or not, survivors of the PRS ordeal are almost our sole source of recruits for our own group; they make up the only people we can be perfectly sure of. Otherwise we have to go through our regular testing procedure, and that takes so many years that we'd be whittled down to nothing if we depended upon it alone.

"You'll remember, for instance, my 'infinity of time' argument, where I tried to sell you on the idea that

179

anything odd that happened to you was to be laid at the door of an extreme violation of chance. That was one of our tests. The argument is ridiculous, but it *sounds* reasonable, and a man who can't see through it will never make a good psi-man. Being a good psi-man takes intelligence and lots of it. It also takes considerable independence of mind, since the psi-man has to live with the knowledge that he's vastly different from most of his fellow men, at least at present; he has to be comfortable with that knowledge, but at the same time he can't allow himself to get a swelled head over it. You'll remember that I insisted that violations of chance occur all the time—extreme violations. Daily experience will tell you that that isn't so; but I said very forcibly that it was so. If you had taken my word for it—but, you didn't."

"Is this why you told me to see an analyst, too?" Danny said. "You certainly sounded serious about it."

"I was serious, Danny. Not all hallucinations, visions, and so on add up to the possession of psi powers. Sometimes people who are in serious psychological trouble develop the idea that they are becoming psychic, or telepathic, or something like that. Here, let me give you a graphic example. Do you know Marc Lyons?"

The name was vaguely familiar. "Doesn't he write detective stories?" Danny said finally.

"Yes, he does, but he's also a science fiction writer. Some years ago he wrote a short novel in which ESP figured—very inaccurately, by the way, for he's not a psi-man and I see no signs that he'll ever become one. But it was a fair story and he sold it to one of the science
180

fiction magazines. Ten days after it was printed he got
a letter from a reader which he showed to me—he has
no idea that I'm a psi-man or that there is such a thing,
he just thought I'd be amused. Actually, I find it tragic;
but it's a sample of what I mean. Here it is."

Sean produced a piece of blue-ruled notebook paper
and handed it to Danny. It said:

Mr. M. Lions,
NYCity, Ny.
Dear Sir,
　　Re:—The Walkers In The Way—
　　Your article in "Mind Wrenching Stories" of
December intrigued me considerably since the
experiences parallel mine.
　　For about 15 years I was a Spiritual Advisor
raising 3 sons alone & sufferede excrucitating mi-
graines etc etc continuously—having only about
3 days respite a year. All attendant phenomena in
your treatise have been more or less experience
by me—However believe me I have been definitely honest about my psychic abilities—have
had psychiatric counsels—thought I was going
mad—etc—& have found only 2 or 3 learned
people who really understand me.
　　I can no more stop or control it than I can walk
—it is forever present & I live in a different world
& views events differently

(Here there was a marginal note: "I will be walking
alonga street yet I am up over it somewhere explain
that—")

181

Have a State Organization over 15 years old—
but at present am resting against my will.

A Mrs [here a name and address was given]
can attest to my extreme sensitivity which I cannot help.

It gratifies me that science is beginning to
realize that these things are so because I have
been so misunderstood through no fault of mine.

I will be 54 April 10 & can pass for 10 years
younger—without artificial necessities to—This
gift has been with me ever since I was born &
I know the answer to a question before it is
completed in it's entirety—I have to catch myself
in my utterances at times thinking objectively
"it can't be so" but invariably it is—

Please write to me what books I could find the
facts—I have tried to get some but can not seem
to find it—However if you could enlighten me
to further understand myself scientifically I
would greatly appreciate it.

I have a friends in Wanamakers Philadelphia—
who could tell you of my activities. Mrs [here
another name was given] buyer who phones me
for aid.

Thanking you for writing such an article &
hoping for many more I am—Respectfully
[signature]

PS. Another thing I make up my mind to make a
statement & "something foreign" comes out—I
mean other than I had anticipated—What *is it*—
Who dunit?

Danny handed back the letter. "I see what you mean."

"There are other tests," Sean went on. "We're anxious to know about a man's drinking habits, for instance, since use of the psi powers requires terrific precision of mind, which is the first thing that goes under alcohol. That one's easy to apply, since if a man becomes fuzzy under only one drink or a few beers he's probably fairly safe. And so on.

"I was pretty sure you'd come through on all counts, but there is always the chance, right up to the last minute, that a man will freeze in some stage of his development and become a monotalent, a psychic cripple like the PRS men. I got in touch with Taylor very early—he's the senior member of our group, and an expert in bringing out any buried paranoia that may exist in a potential recruit—and it was agreed that one of us, a man you haven't met, should take a post with the Brotherhood and plant the resonator for your use."

"Sean, they burned him," Danny said.

"I know," Sean said levelly. "I—heard it happen, and it had been one of the high probabilities of the assignment from the beginning. We thought it was worth it. If you turned out to be capable of using the resonator to the fullest extent of its possibilities, Taylor agreed with me that you should have every help our group could bring to bear—but not before. I argued that the threshold was set too high, and that if you discovered that the resonator was adjustable at all and used it in one other way than the way it was originally tuned, that should be proof enough. Eventually I won out. We were separated by a good many miles when this decision was

183

reached, and our conversations had to be rather vague. Both Taylor and I became aware early in the game that you could overhear us whenever we were talking about you. But—except for the burning of Cy Nevers—it all came through exactly as we had hoped."

"Then you and Taylor were the 'underground' voices I heard. I finally identified you, but I'd never have guessed that the other man was Taylor, not in fifty billion years. . . . My God, Sean, I feel as if I were sane again for the first time in weeks. I could cut your throat for the hard time you've given me, but I owe you a large wet kiss for tonight."

Sean ducked, chuckling.

"But seriously, Sean: what about Doc Todd? He's been working like a dog for years on this whole problem, and furthermore he's worked out a lot of the answers—worked them out the hard way, because he hasn't a flicker of psi ability himself. I'd be nowhere without him. Surely he deserves some consideration from you people, even though he'll never be a psi-man."

"He's got it," Sean said. "Every human being is a unique problem, Danny. We all come to the psi powers in our own special ways; Todd's isn't yours or mine, and can't be treated as if it were. As a matter of fact, that's an odd question coming from you, Danny. Can't you of all people estann the outcome of Todd's work?"

"I don't want to try," Danny said. "I haven't used any psi faculty since I got away from the PRS. I'm afraid they'll detect it."

"Of course they will. Where have I parked my head?
184

My contempt for them sometimes makes me forget that they have real and dangerous abilities. Furthermore, they've reached a point now where we are going to have to mess them up more than somewhat, and do it fast and clean, too. We'd better stop talking and start moving."

"Where to?"

"To the hide-out across the river, the place where the syndicate took you. We have to wind up your sequence. We should arrive in time enough to see the end of Dr. Todd's search, too, if we succeed, but it's going to be tough to do. Is your truck parked outside?"

"Yes, but I think it's about out of gas."

"I'll run it," Sean said, stripping himself of his robe. "I haven't tried it yet, but it should be possible to run a reciprocating engine without fuel, by bleeding off the gravitic moment of alternate cylinders. Keeler ran his 'mystery engine' that way, Taylor thinks, though I'm sure Keeler didn't know it himself."

"Doesn't the PRS keep posted on you pretty continuously, Sean?"

"As much as possible, I suppose. They may not suspect me of harboring you, though—and even if they do, they're scared of me and won't interfere until driven to it. I'm counting on their not knowing what I'm up to until it's too late; that's why I'm not telling you the whole deal now." He put out lights and opened the door. "We'll have to hurry—a new sequence has already started, and unless we wind up yours properly the new one will replace it."

"That's bad?"

185

"Very bad," Sean said. "The new one starts a chain which eventually gives the PRS full control. To use your bridge-game analogy, Danny, right now you're trumps. If we don't play you now, we'll never have another chance."

chapter fourteen

THE ACE OF EAGLES

The truck purred through the darkness, Danny guiding it, Sean sitting beside him in the cab, apparently inactive. Since there was no gasoline exploding in the cylinders, the engine made virtually no noise; otherwise its performance seemed no different than before, unless it was perhaps a little smoother and more genteel than a truck engine had any right to be.

The lights of passing cars picked out Sean's sharp features. He was still smiling, but there was little mockery in the smile now. He seemed to be taking real pleasure in the small task of keeping the fuelless motor operating, as if his intimate relationship with the shuttling pistons were something he had often wanted to experience.

Danny, long harried by the forces aroused against him by his random tests of the psi powers, saw for the first time something of the joy of those powers, saw it glowing in the unusual relaxation of Sean's smile.

"And you can't tell me anything about what's coming, then?"

"Very little," Sean said. "We've been working for a long time on two problems, both of considerable importance. One of them, as a matter of fact, is probably the oldest and toughest problem man has had, and so it's the one where the solution still seems farthest away. It doesn't apply to the present situation, but you'll be hearing plenty about it later; either Taylor or I will give you a rundown on what's been done so far."

"And the other one?"

"That's the one we may have to use tonight," Sean said. "We're looking for some psychic equivalent of nuclear fission. We've known for a long time that the behaviour of electrons betrays a kind of thought. I don't mean to imply that electrons are sentient, but simply that their behaviour is analogous to that of sentient creatures. Everything Dirac and Heisenberg and their colleagues have done on electronic motion and position shows something that, for want of a more applicable term, we call thought.

"Our experience with the psi principles shows that the Bohr wave-atom has, in effect, a psychology of its own. And as long ago as three centuries, through the initial studies of the behaviour of mobs, we found our first inkling that this electronic psychology was mirrored in human behaviour."

Danny guided the truck through the complicated, graceful approaches to the Kingsway Bridge and paid the toll. "What kind of human behaviour?" he said.

"Mob action, first of all—and secondly, schizoid behaviour. We think now that most forms of schizophrenia represent a splitting of the personality into psi and non-psi
188

groups, sometimes dozens of them in the same brain. The psi-associated groups become totally divorced from all cortical activity and live in the psi centers exclusively; the cortical groups develop voluntary activity unmodified by any psi control or any access to it. Theoretically this kind of dissociation can go on until there's nothing left of the personality at all, though what the consequences would be in a person with fully active psi-centers, a psi-man, it's hard to imagine. In any event, we've been looking for a way to induce this kind of splitting and we expect to find it very soon now. Just incidentally, it would be a terrible weapon."

"Cripes, Sean, somebody's anticipated your secret. Franz Werfel's last book has a war scene in it where mental bombardment is used."

. "Why not?" Sean said. "You don't get to be a serious novelist without some understanding of these things. We certainly don't object to such descriptions. They often contain clues which help us along." He turned his head suddenly. "Look out, Danny, the driveway is only half a mile from here. Better douse your lights and we'll go the rest of the way on foot. Don't lose the resonator whatever you do. And there's one other hint I can give you about what's coming: *give Todd plenty of elbow room.* Understand?"

"More or less. I'll bear it in mind."

"Good. I'm going to kill the engine now. All set?"

"Sure."

The engine sputtered air and died. Sean opened the door of the truck and got out. Danny followed him. It

189

was very quiet, with crickets underlining the silence. There were thousands of stars.

"How come they came back here after the fight with the Pinks?" Danny whispered.

"You don't have to whisper yet. Anyhow they know *I'm* coming at least. As for the Pinks, they're of the opinion that they won the fight and cleaned the place out. They have eight or ten dupes to show for it, and some very firm opinions as to what happened which they don't suspect are not their own."

"Did you—"

"No, I didn't. The PRS is out here now, Danny. They've been following your every move for days, ever since they first encountered you. When you teleported yourself out of the garret here they nearly had hysterics. They took over at once, blanketed the cops to prevent their arriving at your apartment for at least an hour, and sent some of the smaller fry to get Todd and bring him here. The Pinks were given a little mental manhandling and sent home. I don't know what happened to the boss gambler; I suppose he got away, since he's still valuable to them despite his serious underestimation of you; anyhow he no longer counts, because the PRS is now handling things directly."

Danny whistled. "They're big medicine when they exert themselves," he said.

"Yes, they are. They aren't sure you're alive, but they're baiting the trap with Todd just in case you are—they expect you to think that the gamblers are still out here and giving the old man a going-over, and they expect you to try to get him out."

190

"They'd be right, but for you."

Sean stepped off the road, crossed the culvert, and clambered a fence into a field of timothy, beckoning to Danny. "I'm blanketing you at the moment, and I hope they'll think I'm alone. If they try to bluff me we'll have just that much more time in which to work. I think they will."

Danny felt a faint glow of warmth in his shirt pocket and fumbled in it for the resonator. The little metal egg was the source of the heat. "The resonator's heating up," he reported.

"Stand still."

After a moment Sean said, "How is it now?"

"I think it's cooling off. Yes, it is."

"Better put it in neutral. Evidently they've put out an impedance field. We don't want to burn it out. You'll need it."

Danny sprang the case open and found the control buttons in the starlight. He returned them to neutral with the screwdriver Sean had given him, feeling the manifold horizons of the serial universe closing in about him. It was a curiously unpleasant feeling, although only a week ago the confinement of his mind to a single "frame" would have seemed normal to him.

"That's good," Sean said. "That blankets you twice as efficiently as I can at this range, and it avoids the risk of their catching me at it."

"I don't like it," Danny complained.

"I don't blame you. But it shouldn't be necessary long."

Abruptly Danny saw the house, long, low and lightless against the spangled sky, with a smudge of forest behind

191

it. He discovered it so suddenly that it seemed almost to have sprung at him out of the Milky Way.

"I'll go right on in," Sean murmured. "I'm going to stage a big confrontation scene and get them to tell me where they have Todd. That's the secret of dealing with Sir Lewis; apply plenty of bluster. You give me a start, and then sneak up under that window that's just to the right of the chimney—you'll see it as you get closer. Don't worry about being caught. They have a complete clairvoyant lookout covering this area, so they won't bother using the eyes God gave them—and with the resonator in neutral, no ESP sense can spot you."

His teeth flashed in the radiant night. "It's funny—I can see you, but I'm so used to estanning people that I can hardly believe you're there myself. You're something new in the world, Danny—you're psychically invisible!"

He turned and looked toward the house. "Good luck, Danny," he said. "Do whatever you do with confidence; you *are* the Jack of Eagles, and probably due for a promotion. If it comes through, remember that you can call on Taylor for help."

Without allowing Danny a moment for a reply—had Danny had one to make, for the curious speech communicated nothing to Danny but an unfocussed chill of foreboding—he strode away swiftly toward the house. Danny lost sight of him almost at once.

Danny stood patiently in the sweet-smelling timothy. He missed the psi faculties, though they had brought him little but grief thus far. The sensation of being directly in touch with the basic fabrics of the serial universe, the

192

multiple laminations of space-time, had been reassuring, a new order of reality. But being, as Sean had put it, psychically invisible was no mean advantage. Danny began to understand better the magnitude of the risk Sean had taken in giving the PRS the resonator.

Still, Sean's precognition of the results had indicated that the PRS would be unable to use the little device. Danny wished fervently that he could estann, if only for a split second, the probable end of this sequence of events—Sean had been so indefinite about it. It was ridiculous, after all this long struggle toward full realization of the psi powers, to be in a spot which forbade him to use them.

A rectangle of yellow light opened in the hulking shadow of the house, silhouetting Sean's slim body and a chunkier one. Indistinct murmurs drifted over the timothy; the chunky man in the door way gesticulated; then, he moved out of the way and Sean went in. Then the light was cut off again.

Danny sprinted toward the spot Sean had indicated. As he got closer, he discovered why he had been unable to see the window from the field: it was covered by metal shutters.

There were, however, several slits between the shutters big enough for him to see through. It gave into the same room that Danny had seen before in the lodge, the one where the boss gambler and Tooey had questioned him.

The gambler was not at the big desk now. Instead, it was occupied by a smaller man with a fringe of red hair and a bald spot. That pate looked extremely familiar, but the man's back was to Danny. It wasn't the flowery

N   193 white poll of Sir Lewis Carter—and every other PRS man Danny had seen had been cowled.

Another player who up to now had been carrying his cards in his sleeve.

The door across the room opened, and Sean came in. The chunky man was with him, but he seemed glad to be rid of his charge. The man at the desk looked up.

Sean looked back and smiled. His lips moved. The man at the desk nodded. Danny pressed his forehead hard against the painted metal of the shutters, and was rewarded with a just-distinguishable murmuring.

"This is a pleasant surprise," Sean was saying. "The Brotherhood must be desperate."

"The Brotherhood knows what it's doing," the other man said. "Speak up, Hennessy. My t-time is valuable."

"Not to me," Sean said. "You're holding Dr. Todd here. We want him released."

"We know nothing about your Dr. T-Todd. You know as well as I d-do that we have n-nothing to do with p-p-p-parapsychologists. We decided long ago that any program ag-g-gainst them would speedily convince them that they were on the r-right track."

The stutter was unmistakable. Danny looked around the room for the incredibly battered hat that went with it, the hat that had been an office joke for as long as the oldest Delta sub-editor could remember. It was there, all right, on a halltree in the far corner behind the door.

"All events are unique," Sean said. "Todd is here. Do you think you could hide that from *me?*"

The other man was silent for a long moment. "No,"

194

he said at last. "Suppose t-Todd *is* here? Are you going to pretend that you could f-find him?"

"No," Sean responded, surprisingly. "I hadn't expected to find you in charge here. The last I heard, you were hiding under the bed until you were sure Caiden was out of the picture; I expected to have to deal with Sir Lewis, who would have hidden Todd in some obvious place. I've no doubt that you've got the old man squirreled away in some series it would take me a million years to locate. I don't propose to fritter away my youth beating my way through the Crusades or the caliphate of Mukkad Bejh in hopes of seeing Todd."

"I didn't think you would," the man at the desk said sardonically. "You w-won't find him in the Siege of Trebizond, or in the t-Teapot Dome incident, either. Any other g-guesses?"

"I said I wasn't going to try," Sean said. "Produce him."

"Drop d-dead."

For a moment, Danny thought that Sean had done exactly that. He bent double in the middle and fell side-wise, his eyes closed, his face set in iron lines of pain, and disappeared in front of the desk. The other man rose triumphantly to his feet; but he was only halfway up when his desk rose with him, teetering in midair.

Under it, Danny could see Sean again. He was sprawled on the carpet, propping himself up with both hands. His head was held up with an obvious effort, as if it had suddenly turned to lead; the cords in his neck stood out like cables. But his eyes were bright and burning, and bore directly upon the other man.

The desk rose higher, made a sudden, abortive lunge

toward the redhead, and then turned instead upon its long axis, dumping the inkpot into the redhead's lap. The redhead swore.

Sean grinned, but he was sweating heavily. "Why, Mall," he said. "If your god-fearing publishers could hear you now—"

The desk bobbed and began to move, slowly, ponderously, toward Sean. The redhead turned, edging out from behind it. It was Mall, all right. The ink made a large black stain in one of his trouser-legs. He was sweating, too; but there was no doubt of the fact that he knew he was winning.

Frantically Danny opened the resonator, building an electron field as he did so. With all ESP shut off it was impossible for him to tell just how heavy a field would be needed to handle the desk; if he overdid it, Mall would know at once that Sean had help. He had to work entirely by guess. As soon as the PK field was ready to go, he turned one set-screw, just enough to pass a telekinetic projection.

Nothing semed to happen. The two men still faced each other, struggling for control of the heavy desk. Danny could not believe that it could be that massive; he could not sense its mass, since the shield around him blocked his ESP powers as well as those of anyone else who might be searching for him, but the PK field he had projected should have sufficed to move any ordinary piece of furniture with great alacrity.

There was only one answer: Mall's own PK powers were enormous—greater in sum than Danny's and Sean's together.

196

No—not quite greater. Gradually, the wobbling object canted toward Mall. This time, the lamp fell off it, its shade bouncing and rolling away as it hit the rug. In the unmodified glare of the bare bulb Sean and Mall were as harshly shadowed as if they had been cut from granite.

The desk continued to advance inexorably upon Mall, backing him toward the window. If he could be grabbed as soon as his back hit the glass—

Danny pried frantically at the shutters. They refused to move.

"I don't like to use force," Sean gritted. "But your error in trying to kill me was a serious one, Mall. Almost as serious an error as marooning Todd in a sigma-sequence. And he's in a sigma-sequence, Mall, because not even you could force him back into the past, into some historical series. You've got him hidden in some probable future, and you're going to regret it—if you live."

"Prove it," Mall gasped.

"Shortly. You're a joke of a psi-man, Mall. When you put Todd in a sigma-sequence, you cut your own throat. Don't you know that he's on the verge of mastering the psi powers? Don't you know that being taken out of his own everyday series was all the clue he needed? *Don't you know you're going to die?*"

"*Carter!*" Mall screamed. "Aubrey! Elliott! Schaum! *Carter!*"

The desk inched forward. Danny's bleeding fingers slipped on the cold metal, but this time the shutter gave a little.

Mall's eyes darted about the room. When he saw the

fallen lamp, he cried out hoarsely with triumph, and at the same time the desk charged at him like a geometrical mastodon. He paid no attention; he looked at the lamp—

The lamp bulb burst. A thin wedge of electrical green shot through the sudden darkness. Sean cried out.

There was a heavy slam as the desk hit the floor. Something passed Danny in a whisper, something he knew, something he knew he would never know again. Then it was gone, and Danny felt tears streaming down his face. Sean—Sean—

The shutter screeched suddenly and swung open; at the same instant, the room door was kicked back and Sir Lewis' bulky shadow was cast into the dark room. The green beam wavered and went out. Nearly blinded, Danny threw a shoe over the windowsill and kicked the glass in.

"What the devil, Mall! Did you get him?"

"I—think s-so. B-but he's still alive. He's g-got a PK field in that desk yet and I heard s-something go through the window."

Danny ground his teeth and backed the resonator into neutral.

"I don't feel any PK field."

"It's g-gone now. It could have b-been residual. But watch out. He's strong—my god but he's s-strong!"

"These high-minded idiots depend too much on themselves," Sir Lewis said. "He could have been nine times as strong as you were, and still be a fool to tackle us all single-handed." He kicked in the darkness until he hit Sean. "There he is. Not a thought in his head; he's dead, Mall."

198

"I don't want him dead; maybe he's j-just out. I've set up a nerve-block in him. Get one of your t-teleports to move him out of here and into the impedance field, and see that he g-gets medical attention. If he does die, we'll have t-Taylor and all the rest of that crowd down on us."

"And Caiden, too."

"Caiden is d-dead. Don't bother your head over him."

"I wouldn't be too sure," Sir Lewis said. "He might not have gone to Hennessy, after all."

"If he survived, he went to Hennessy," Mall said coldly. "The sequence would admit of n-nothing else. And obviously he isn't w-with Hennessy. Next t-time you have a crisis, you'll depend on my p-predictions and handle it yourselves."

"I'm still not satisfied," Sir Lewis grumbled. "But you're the Prytanis here. If you say Caiden's dead, I suppose he has to be dead."

The two went out. Danny waited, scarcely daring to breathe, forgotten tears drying on his face. His foot had been sticking through the broken glass into the room throughout the whole conversation, but neither Sir Lewis nor Mall had so much as looked toward the window.

After a short interval, a tall, spare shadow stuck its head around the door jamb. Sean's body rose from the floor. The shadow disappeared. Sean's body floated after it.

The room was deserted.

Cautiously, Danny withdrew his foot, and raised the sash. A piece of glass tinkled, and he froze. But nothing happened.

He heaved himself up over the sill and clambered into the room. Mall and Carter had thought Sean still alive partly because of Danny's ineffectual PK field in the desk, but also because of the sound of the windowpane breaking; they hadn't bothered to check on whether or not Sean had actually thrown—or telekineticized—something through it from inside, or whether the breaking glass had meant something else.

But Danny knew. The current from the burst bulb-socket had killed Sean; Danny had felt it happen. It had been quick. He wondered what it had been like for Sean to feel Cy Nevers' death, which had been much slower . . .

It hit Danny suddenly, as he stood there in the tense darkness, that Sean had expected just such an outcome; at least, he had anticipated it, for his odd parting speech about Danny's forthcoming "promotion" could have meant nothing else. And from the moment he had found himself confronting Mall instead of Sir Lewis—knowing, as Danny had not known until now, the almost fantastic PK powers Mall could wield—he had known he would lose, even with Danny's belated help.

For that matter, he had known that Mall was one of the key men of the PRS. He had walked into the trap the PRS had set all the same, knowing that he might fall before the man whom he had despised—and watched—for nearly three years in the *Food Chronicler* office.

If Sean were dead, he had died in the expectation that Danny would be able to beat Mall and the PRS by himself. He had named Danny the King of Eagles.

And if he were not dead—though Danny knew that
200

he was—he would expect Danny to go after Todd, and waste no time trying to extricate Sean from a situation Sean had chosen for himself.

Most important of all, he had given Danny an instrumentality which was capable of dealing with the entire problem if Danny used it properly. Up to now, the best uses of the resonator had depended upon its employment to restrict the psi powers. There was no question but that it could also be used to amplify them greatly—and that it was going to have to be used that way before this night was over. Until further notice, however, Danny was going to continue to use it in the way he knew best. In this house of all houses, to be psychically invisible was the best of all possible advantages.

He peered out into the corridor. It was empty, though there was murmuring going on behind a closed door on the other side.

Danny padded along it, looking for the steps to the garret. At a turn at the end of the corridor he ran upon them, just as he had remembered them.

Except that there were far too many of them.

The steps were as distorted as if seen on the surface of a sphere, and they seemed to turn away from each other in every direction. Phantom staircases spiraled into nothingness from each successive riser; farther aloft, there was nothing but a static haze, dimly marked with innumerable shadows and curved planes.

Something strange was going on upstairs. It did not look as though a man could walk up those treads and expect to reach the top.

Todd was up there. But where "up there" might be was

anybody's guess. Here, at last, was a department in which experience counted: the Brotherhood knew enough about the psi forces to do technical tricks with them, while Danny, regardless of how great his native abilities might be, was still a tyro—and, since he lacked the basic technical knowledge of a Todd, he had neither tools nor clues for tackling the mystery.

But wait a minute. He could at least attempt to borrow Todd's brains. The parapsychologist had found the basic PK equation to be identical with a formula well known to ordinary physics: a thing called the Blackett equation, unfamiliar to Danny but apparently not at all esoteric to scientists. And toward the end of the research which the thugs had interrupted, he had been seeking a master formula which would cover both PK and ESP—

And the Blackett equation had contained an uncertainty correction.

Hastily Danny rummaged in the incredible lumber-room of his memory for the relevant material, which he was sure should be there, filed under "Heisenberg—Principle of Indeterminacy." After a second he had it, along with the entire page of Korzybski's *Science and Sanity* on which he had encountered it during his library session. The main formula read:

$$pq-qp=h/2\pi i (1)$$

"where," the visualized text said, "h represents the Planck constant, q the generalized coordinate, p the momentum, 1 stands for the unit matrix, and π and i have the usual meaning."

That was just great. It certainly seemed to have nothing to do with the multifoliate staircase before him; but, ap-

202

parently incomprehensible though it was, he had no other tool to use. Todd had once credited him with a good grasp of elementary physics—now it was up to Danny to prove it.

Grimly he buckled down, his thoughts sliding easily into the blurringly high speed which he had first mastered so long ago in the apartment before he had called Todd back. The left-hand side of the equation, then, could be discounted, since only the right hand side gave it meaning—the expression was not reversible. The sign i stood for the square root of minus one, a definite numerical quantity and hence not truly a variable; the same was true of π. That left nothing but h, and that was a constant—it said so, right there on the remembered page.

But it wasn't!

Planck's constant, as he had been taught in college years ago, was the invariant element in a quantum, the single, indivisible "packet" of energy on which the universe seemed to operate. In our universe, it was a tiny figure, just .00000000000000000000000000000655 erg-seconds; but by the same token, if that basic constant were to change, the entire energy-level of the cosmos would change with it.

That, then, was what the second set-screw in the resonator was for: it "tuned" to different values of h. And on a large scale, it explained what the Brotherhood had done with the stairwell. It had used variations of h as a lever to separate the sequences of the serial universe whose totality made up the main line. Since the PRS men would not be interested in most of the intermediate sequences, they could select out the sequences in which their cause, their part of the plot in Marla's postulated endless movie of time, was most heavily favored; and in the most favorable sequence of all would be the best hiding place for Todd. The quantum-level gaps between such strips would certainly be quite large, easily large enough to be graspable by delicate instruments.

One of the voices behind the closed door became louder, and more stubborn. Danny could not make out the words, but the halting rhythm of the syllables identified Mall. Another voice roared suddenly, and a chair scraped back. Obviously some sort of argument had been in progress—and was now on the verge of breaking up—

Desperation drove him suddenly over the lip of repressed hysteria into a sort of shock, where he found his thoughts moving faster than they had ever gone before, but moving through a freezing, inhuman lack of emotion. The thoughts rushed through his head like figures on a tape, not only rapidly, but bare, stripped. It was perfectly clear to him that the intuitive mathematical leap which he had just performed had been an intellectual feat of a high order for a person without training. The realization did not elate him; he was incapable of feeling elation now. He simply accepted the idea.

By the same token he knew coldly that he did not dare climb that staircase with nothing to go by but the mathematical concept. He fully appreciated that to understand a single mathematical concept does not automatically confer ability to use it. It was, for instance, all very well to say that each one of the steps ahead led to a new level of the serial universe, one where the value Planck's Constant was higher than it had been in the level immediately preceding it—but he was not scientist enough to appreciate the consequences of the change, 204 or to predict them, in immediately practical terms; nor to interpret whatever consequences he did find well enough to know where to go from there, or how to proceed on arrival.

In short, if he simply followed his intuition up those stairs, he would get lost.

And if he went up there steering by some false or incomplete analogy, he would get lost all the faster. It would be a mistake, for instance, to proceed by thinking of the levels of the serial universe as independent, parallel existences; that was a philosophical braincracker of long standing and one which Danny knew had no status in physical reality. Yet the concept of "parallel universes" had so many points of resemblance to the actual situation that it was hard not to be led astray by it.

There was nothing for it but to grasp hold of Marla's movie-film analogy as firmly as possible. Todd had specifically called it "a very good way to think of" the serial universe; that could be counted on to mean that the analogy was not grossly false to the facts. The only danger remaining was that it was incomplete.

Complete it, then—insofar as an analogy can be completed toward the reality it is supposed to stand for. Imagine the stream of time as divided up into an indefinite number of equal segments, like a tapeworm—or a strip of motion picture film. In only one such strip, the actors and the props in each frame would be two-dimensional, and would not seem very real.

Now lay another strip directly on top of the first one, running in the same direction. The actors and the props in the second strip are *almost* the same as those in the

205

first, but not quite identical. They, too, are two-dimensional and nearly unreal. Now a third strip is added to the pile—slightly different from the second strip, more markedly different from the first. Repeat the process with a fourth strip, and a fifth, a sixth, a seventh.

Now bring a light and look *through* the piled strips at a single frame, a single instant of time as it exists in each of the levels of the serial universe. No single image shows through; instead, you see a composite. The slightly differing, mostly unreal and flat objects and actors add up to three-dimensional images, standing there in the three-dimensional space bounded by the edges of the pile of film-strips. The composite images partake of the characteristics of all the individual images.

That seemingly solid composite represented the "real" world, the additive effect of all the levels of the serial universe—the thing Sean had called "the main line," as distinct from the contributing individual "sequences."

But "sequence" suggests time, and motion. There was progression and change from frame to frame in the piled film-strips. Here was the real secret, the recondite core of the serial universe—the difference in time.

Put a hand on top of the piled film-strips, and press down, rather hard. Then move the hand forward half an inch.

The top strip slides the full half inch. The one just under it slides a little less; the strip under that, still slightly less. The very bottom strip may not move at all; but when you hold the light up to the piled strips again, you will see that the discrepancy between the frames in the top strip and those in the bottom one is serious.

The instant which is "now" on the bottom strip has been moved forward in time, a considerable distance, in the top strip.

(To his extreme annoyance, another intuitive flash interrupted Danny's analogy-building at this point. Two years ago, he had happened upon an utterly incomprehensible article by the British physicist J. B. S. Haldane, about a theory of non-Einsteinean relativity which involved a raising of the energy-level of the whole universe as more years were added to the universe's age. Danny had no sooner imaged the sliding of the piled film-strips than Haldane's once recondite concept—he did not remember that Haldane had actually been explaining another man's idea, nor would he have cared if he had—came back to him as the most natural and inevitable of natural laws.)

What, then, had the Brotherhood done? They had separated the film-strips. In that shimmering stairwell, there was no "main line," no aggregate of strips to add up to one composite reality. Instead, each of the strips took on its own individual existence, with all the slight differences between strips freed to assert themselves independently, just as if each strip were a "main line" all in itself.

Every time Danny went from one step to another, he would be snapped into another world. Not an unreal world, but not a real one either; simply a nearly-fictional world which could become fact only by being lumped with its sibling half-truths.

And—he would go forward in time. Each new half-world

would be slewed slightly farther into the future than the one preceding it. How far "slightly" might be—seconds, or centuries—he had no idea, but the chances favored long jumps more than short ones. In normal space-time, one second and 186,000 miles are equivalent distances; there was no reason to believe that "slight" variations in such a basic factor as the energy-level of the cosmos would be any less spectacular.

That, then, was how it was; but knowing that made mounting those steps seem inconceivably more dangerous than before. All of the sequences in which the PRS had an advantage would offer obvious dangers—but even more than that, the higher one mounted from sequence to sequence, the more remote from the main line of probability one would travel, so that the closer to the garret Danny got, the more likely he would be to find himself, at the first false step, cut off in some world of If which he would never be able to leave again . . .

Still, the resonator should help. If he kept the first set-screw in neutral, keeping his mind confined to a single "frame," his chances of going astray from sequence to sequence would be held at a minimum, and that setting would also tend to winnow out the close-lying sequences which were only transitional between those where Todd might be hidden. A careful focussing of the second set-screw should spread his mind far enough along the Planck axis to show him the course he should follow from level to level—

A door opened behind him. The voices came out of the room, louder now, but still distorted.

Danny grimaced. He had no choice. He took out the resonator and twisted the second screw. The stairwell rippled.

"For Christ's sake—Carter, *Carter!* Get out here—it's Caiden, *and he's going to tackle the sigma-sequence—*"

chapter fifteen

THE SIX TOMORROWS

Danny heard, but he paid no attention. Every fraction of his concentration was bent upon the resonator. Gently, microscopically, he turned the second set-screw. More than half of the phantom staircases had already fogged into nothing but faint traceries. Of those that remained visible, six were solid and clamored to be climbed. He advanced the set-screw a little, a very little more.

"Throw that thing out of his hand—"

"I can't, it won't budge. It's pinned to one frame, somehow. Carter, you incredible fool, you gave him the machine—"

"At your orders. Burn him, then, quick—where the hell is Schaum—"

That was no good; now he had about twenty staircases back again. He edged the button away; again there were six staircases. Then that was what it would have to be; six. One of them led to Todd.

"No time—rush him—"

Danny took the first step.

ONE

The stairs vanished.

So did the house, and with it the darkness of the corridor.

Danny was standing on the meadow, alone. But even the meadow was altered. The timothy was gone. The terrain was lumpy, and dotted with stubble. It was freezing cold; and barren, except for a few monster stems waving in the wind, stems so huge that it was hard to believe that they could ever have been timothy.

A few stones, scattered around Danny, showed him where the house was supposed to be—or where it had been, before something had happened to it.

There was still a smell of timothy, but it was much too strong. The barren stank of timothy—rotten.

Behind the ruins of the house was a bare forest of dead trees, their bark peeling scrofulously from dead trunks. Many of them had fallen and their stumps and stems were punky, though the forest was still as much a scrub growth as it had ever been, and there was no visible reason why such young trees should fall, even in winter.

The sky was gray and clouded. Toward the north, where the city should have been, there was only a twisting of fog. A black bird, like a crow but much bigger, circled and circled in the damp, heavily cold wind. It saw Danny and cried out. The cry echoed and echoed over the moor.

Ke-a. . . . Ke-a.

There was no other sound; no stirring of leaves, no insect

211

noises, nothing at all but the cry of the bird and an occasional sigh of branches.

Bewildered, Danny turned back toward the house. A little of the stairway was still standing, and so was almost all the chimney. The rest of the stones lay at random in the dead stubble, as if the whole house had been blown outward from its center years ago and had never been visited since.

Ke-a. . . . Ke-a. . . .

Tentatively, Danny tried to find some telepathic evidence that something was alive here. Nothing came through. The lack of insect noises was real; there were no insects. The landscape was dead, blasted.

He reached out for the bird—

It was long moments later when he realized that he had nothing left in his stomach to empty; but he kept on retching. He was shaking with terror. He knew that the bird was circling lower and lower, watching his weakness, its bill nibbling tentatively in mid-air in anticipation of his eyes, but he was helpless to rid his memory of that one contact.

The bird was intelligent; almost as intelligent as a dog. It was hungry. It had not fed for days, and the last creature it had stripped had not been a man for months . . .

He coughed and straightened up. Alerted, but not in the least alarmed, the black bird wheeled skyward again to wait.

Ke-a. . . . Ke-a.

There was nothing alive here but Danny and the hoarse black bird. Even the bird had known that. The pall of disaster enveloped not only the house but the world—whether from war or plague he did not know, nor could the bird. But the bird did not care. It wanted Danny's eyes. It had been a long time since the bird had found a creature weak enough to be tricked into looking skyward when the bird called . . .

Danny looked down, swallowing. The stubble was all around his feet, though he was still standing in what should have been the hallway of the house. The sundered steps were still ahead of him, though he had already ascended one of them—in the sequence where he belonged.

Of course. This was only one of the infinite number of overlapping sequences whose totality made the real world. It was neither wholly unreal, nor more than fractionally real. New sequences were starting every instant. One of them, Sean had said, would give the PRS full control of the future if it were allowed to establish itself—if it were allowed to come closer to the main line.

It would be in that sequence that Todd would be hidden, for the PRS would hope that Sean's cohorts would be forced to see the sequence realized in order to get Todd back—and of course a sequence where the PRS was in full control would be the safest place for a prisoner.

Danny had mounted the steps into the first of the PRS' favorable sequences. For that reason, the steps now before him still seemed unmounted; the first step which he had climbed did not exist here, because he had already passed it; it did not belong to this sequence, but to the one he had just left.

Ke-a, ke-a . . .

Danny looked grimly around. So this was the *most* probable outcome of the PRS' manipulations! A world devas-

tated except for a hoarse black bird, the last of its kind . . .
a world in which not even one human being, let alone
Todd, could be kept hidden for an instant. It was not a
promising testimonial.

Ke-a—

Danny looked up to see where the ruined staircase broke
off. There was nothing beyond it but the gray sky; but it
was a signal, a finger-post, that told him he had not yet
climbed far enough—

Ke-a, ke-a! The enormous black thing, vicious, wingless,
torpedoed, needle-led, plunged at his face, its little mind
screaming with triumphant cunning. Danny threw his arm
over his eyes and lunged, staggering, sick, up the second
step.

TWO

For an instant he thought he had stepped into midair.
The gray sky persisted, and wheeled all around him. He
flailed for a handhold, and got nothing; he was falling
and—

A strong hand took him by the forearm, and another put
his own hand firmly on something tubular, metallic, and
cold.

"Easy, old man. The wind is bad up here; you have to
hang on to the handrail or you'll get blown off."

The voice was reassuring, friendly. Gradually, Danny
was able to rid himself of his dizziness. Even so, it was
hard to find anything in sight which would anchor him to
some ground.

He began with the handrail, which was simply a shining

214

pipe which curved away from him on both sides, describing a circle scarcely big enough to hold three men. The rail, in turn, went around a tiny metal platform, which swayed back and forth atop a single reed of metal nearly two hundred feet from the earth. Once he saw where the ground was, and realized the minuteness of the target onto which he had stepped, he became dizzy all over again, and nearly dropped the resonator in seeking a fresh grip on the platform railing.

"Hang on. You'll get used to it." The man next to him released him, cautiously. Danny canted his head to look at him.

It was Sean. Or—no, it was only fractionally Sean; a coarser version of the King of Eagles, oblivious of the ramifications of the universe which had been Sean's life's blood. But the resemblance was too marked to be ignored.

Below, there was an encampment, stretching for miles and miles. Tiny men scurried through it. Half the forest—which looked much bigger and more mature—had been cut down to make rude barracks. The city was still visible to the north, though its silhouette was quite wrong; it contained several tall buildings which were no part of it in Danny's world. A cleared field to the south was even more conspicuous; on it, ten identical projectiles, like shining metal fish, lay in cradling webs of girders; an eleventh stood on its tail fins, being serviced by a Gantry crane.

The platform swayed like a tulip in the wind. The man who looked like Sean shifted his rifle to the other shoulder. "All right now?" he said.

Danny nodded numbly.

"I didn't see you come up or I'd have been ready for you.

215

These teleporters are goddam careless about the way they pitch a man 200 feet in the air. First thing I knew, there you were."

"Thanks," Danny said. "I was dizzy."

"Sure. It hits you that way the first time. I'll stick with you for a while, until you get used to it."

Danny looked at the soldier wonderingly. "I'm your relief, aren't I?" he said.

"Sure, but I'm in no hurry. I know how it is when you're first put on guard detail; I was green at it not so long ago, myself. Don't worry about me; I'll holler for transportation to ground the minute I want to go. Where's your rifle?"

"I don't know," Danny said. "I guess I must have dropped it."

"You couldn't have dropped it. They must have forgotten to send it up with you. They get more careless every day. I'm Sean Hennessy; what's your name?"

"Danny Caiden."

"Hmm. Seems to me—no, I guess not." The soldier leaned on the railing, looking down toward the clearing, shifting his rifle easily. "Look at them," he said. "What a lot of hell in pretty packages. Carrick says they'll be firing five of them tonight, but I think it's just another latrine rumor. You heard anything?"

"Not a thing," Danny said truthfully.

"Me neither. Cripes, it's cold up here."

"I'm all right now. Why don't you—"

Something went overhead in the gray sky, with a noise like a police whistle amplified a million times. It was going too fast to be visible; from the sound, Danny suspected that it had already gone by long before he had heard it.
216

"There's one that's not for us," the man who looked like Sean said conversationally. "You know, Danny, sometimes I wish I was in the Teletroops after all. At least I hear that they never get guard details."

"I don't think I'd go for it," Danny said.

"Maybe not. Still it hands me a laugh every time I think of the way the experts got turned out wrong again. All the atom bombs and other stuff were supposed to make the infantry out of date. Then they get this teleport thing and wham! The infantry's top dog again and gets shot back and forth around the world like so many cablegrams."

Suddenly it added up. The PRS was a factor, back on the main line, in the world munitions business. In a sequence where the PRS could no longer keep the secret of teleportation, inevitably it would put that secret to military use; in short, turn it into an asset of Consolidated Warfare Service, to be merchandised like a canister of gas or an athodyd. And under such circumstances, the PRS would be more determined than ever to keep the world in a perpetual state of war or near-war, insofar as it lay within the power of the Brotherhood to accomplish it.

This sequence, then, was markedly closer to the PRS' most favored sequence, the one in which Todd was hidden. But it was still a long distance away, for it was a virtual certainty that in that favored sequence the general public would know nothing at all about the psi powers.

That settled it. He had to go on. Tentatively—for the memory of the hoarse black bird was still vivid and horrible—he looked up.

How do you climb empty air? He was already as high as he could go.

No, not quite. There was still the guard rail.

"Oh, oh," the man who looked like Sean said. "Something's up. I hope I'm wrong about what it is. Look at them."

A swarm of tiny men had burst out of the barracks. While Danny watched, they melted into the woods. On the field, more tiny men fled wildly away from the shining torpedoes. It was as if the entire camp had suddenly been ordered to stage a demonstration of organized panic—like the scattering of movie extras before the eruption of a plaster-of-Paris Pompeii. A siren wavered, distantly.

"Hell-bomb," the man who looked like Sean said, with complete calm. "Don't know what good it does them to run. The ESP watch hasn't called a dud yet. So long, Danny."

Frantically, Danny heaved one foot up onto the guard rail.

"*Hey!*" the man who looked like Sean shouted. "You crazy fool, you'll be dead anyhow in a—"

Danny lunged upward and stepped off onto the empty air.

THREE

The soldier's voice snapped out of existence. Danny was enveloped in a humming dusk. His next step struck a solid surface at once, and after only two or three steps he had his balance back.

The camp was gone—both gone from around Danny, and gone from its own sequence by now, obliterated along with everything else within a radius of fifty miles. The fact that it was only partially real did not prevent Danny from

218

feeling a thoroughly real hatred for the PRS. Those men had been real to themselves, and no more anxious to die en masse in a hydrogen-bomb blast than any man on the main line.

Anything the PRS had a hand in meant suffering. It was a fact Danny carried with him now, and one he meant to have in the forefront of his mind when he met the PRS again.

He looked around. High over his head, a vaulted ceiling arched its back, supported by smoothly-curved, graceful buttresses of dark metal. The ceiling sheltered something immense and dark and throbbing with power, a great enigmatic mass which rested on the earth some hundreds of feet away from Danny. The building itself seemed to be as big as a zeppelin hangar, and was designed rather like one, too; but that black mass was no zeppelin, nor anything else that Danny recognized.

The curving sides of the hangar were interrupted regularly by tall, narrow windows. Through them, Danny could see sunlight, and the pointed spires of the distant city, again familiar but changed; here they had both more grace and more delicacy. Along the floor, which really did seem to be earth and nothing more, ran long, intersecting trails like the marks of caterpillar treads.

Which, Danny discovered immediately, was exactly what they were. There were no men in the hangar. The throbbing black machine was being tended by other machines, things like half-tracks without cabs, fenders, bumpers or lights, but equipped with deft and complicated metal arms which were carried, when not in use, folded mantis-like across what would have been the radiator of a

219

half-track. They were very quiet, and they moved with purpose and with obvious intelligence. They were easily the most fascinating mechanisms Danny had ever seen in his life—and they were certainly most unlike Hollywood's versions of what a robot would look like.

One of them glided silently out from behind Danny and started to pass him. He watched it, wondering whether or not he should be afraid.

The machine seemed to be struck by a similar indecision. It paused and sat there, its front wheels canted toward Danny, but its jointed chassis still aligned forward, as if unable to decide whether to turn back or to proceed.

Then its treads began to move slowly backwards. The robot backed away in a new direction and then came forward again. Its front end was still not "looking" directly at Danny when it stopped, and Danny realized that there was no reason why it had to do its looking from its front end. It was simply poised in a position which would allow it to move in any direction with a minimum of waste energy.

"You are in danger here," the robot said. Its voice was neither metallic nor inexpressive; simply matter-of-fact. "It is forbidden that humans enter the plant. There is harmful radiation."

"I'm sorry," Danny said. "I didn't know."

"You should return if you are human," the robot said. "You do not seem to be, however. Your brain is a new type to me. Have the brain-builders decided to dispense with the psi-mechanisms? No such decision is recorded in the matrix-engine."

220

"No," Danny said. "I'm human. I'm shielded, that's all. Evidently you have access to psi information here, too."

"Of course. We have had it for years, that is well known. I myself spoke with the greatest parapsychologist of them all not ten days after I was made. It is a source of satisfaction; not every robot can say he talked with Todd."

Danny jumped. Todd here? Wait a minute—something was decidedly screwy. This sequence was miles away from anything the PRS would set going. For one thing, it seemed to be both peaceful and prosperous, and the psi powers the general property of all.

"Yes, I did," the machine said, a note of something suspiciously like petulance in its voice. "Actually and literally. I was connected directly to his casket in the matrix-engine, and he instructed me himself. Naturally it was not by his own decision, but I felt honored to have been put into contact with him at all; it is rare that any entity is allowed to make contact with the caskets."

"I see," Danny said; and he was afraid that he did. There was always overlapping between the sequences. This one had a Todd in it, just as the previous one had had a Sean— or a sort of a Sean. It probably also had a sort of a Danny Caiden in it.

"Could I talk with Todd?"

"No," the machine said. It sounded offended. "No human, except the Brothers, may talk with Todd or any of the parapsychologists. Only the machines may contact the caskets, and then only for instruction."

A benevolent despotism, then—the kind of thing the PRS would set going if it had to convince a large population that its motives were good. Still not optimum from the

PRS' point of view, for it would involve a lot of compromise with other people's ideas of what constituted benevolence—the machine before him, for instance, obviously had had built into it an attitude of tolerant concern toward the welfare of humans; only the entombing of parapsychologists and other dangerous humans, their incorporation into a computer as helpless and probably normally unconscious components of a master informational system, showed the PRS' thumbprint naked.

But the PRS would prefer not to have to compromise, just as it would prefer this kind of spurious benevolence to a world utterly devastated or under threat of devastation from instant to instant; and above all, it would prefer utter secrecy to any arrangement which allowed anyone but the Brothers to share in psi knowledge.

Danny felt a queer pang of regret. Even under the PRS, this sequence had its points. The discriminating, decorous intelligence of the robot had no parallel in the blindly destructive null-personalities of even the most advanced machines on the main line; he was a little sorry that, if he was successful in reaching the top of this infernal climb, no such machine would be likely to appear in any real future.

And yet—it might. None of the sequences were entirely unreal, and this one was comparatively close to the main line. The robot had a chance for survival in the still-possible future, even if the PRS were destroyed rafter and roof.

"Well," Danny said, "I'll be—shuffling along. Thanks for your courtesy. I've got to go up a step; do you mind if I step on your tread?"

"You are climbing a sigma sequence?" the machine said.

"That explains your presence here; I had been unable to reconcile it. I am sorry to hear it; some of us have suspected that we were not of a very high order of probability, but doubt was always possible."

"It's still possible," Danny said warmly. "I'm from the main line, and you're quite close to it. From what I've seen of you, you'll survive in the real future. That is, you will unless I get stopped somewhere along the line; I don't give you much chance if I am stopped."

"I know that," the machine said calmly. "I have orders to destroy anyone who appears along a sigma sequence. I have delayed doing so because it appeared to me that what you say about our survival is so. I will continue to delay until you escape; but I would advise you not to enter the next quantum-level. There is no Earth there."

"No Earth!"

"No," said the machine. "It will have been vaporized. A premature detonation of the carbon cycle, which was being—or will be being—tested by the Brothers in an attempt to resist a rising underground of psi-men, threatening the world-wide dungeon they had made there. Nor is there even any solar system there, for the shock-wave of radiation from the explosion of the Earth caused the sun to go nova. There is nothing there but an expanding cloud of boiling gas, like the Crab Nebula."

"My god," Danny said. He felt sick again. "What can I do? I'll have to go back down—and now that I come to think of it, I don't even know how to do that. Can't you help me?"

"No," the machine said. "I am violating my instructions by refraining from killing you. But it is not necessary to

223

take a physical upward step to go from sequence to sequence. If you did that, you would be precipitated into the nebular sequence. Cannot you teleport yourself across the gap?"

"Can't risk it," Danny said, wiping his brow distractedly. "I'd be detected."

The machine sat silent and motionless in the humming hall. When it was not speaking, it was hard for Danny to believe in its sentience. Finally it said:

"It is also forbidden me to use psi functions except in the operation of the matrix-engine. However, you are a formulation out of the matrix-series which prevails here, and cannot but be a disturbing factor. I will cancel you out. I estann that they will junk me for it, for the reasoning is full of gaps; but for the sake of our participation in the future, however small it may be—"

Danny was given no time to analyze the robot's proposition, let alone to decide whether or not he wanted to be cancelled out. Though the robot did not move, the great hangar vanished.

FOUR

FIVE

Four inches from the end of his nose, a glittering web-work hung. He could see nothing else. He tried to move, but the webwork flowed smoothly, yielding a little, but holding him as a whole just where he was. It allowed him to look down, but only far enough to discover that the glowing net sheathed his whole body, like a fiery cocoon. It gave enough to allow him to breathe—and that was all.

A harsh voice said, *"Gotcha!"*

Danny struggled, but it did him no good. The owner of the voice waited a good long time to make sure of it.

Then, very tentatively, the glowing, immaterial web-work dimmed a little. Danny stood still. Eventually, the owner of the voice seemed satisfied. The dimming resumed, accelerated; the webwork crawled, and seemed to be evaporating.

At the end it was gone without trace. A tall, hawknosed man with an unruly shock of blue-black hair was opposite Danny, leaning against a table on the other side of a small, low-ceilinged room. In his hand he held a pistol-like object, surmounted by a small square of mirror neatly bisected by cross-hairs.

In the little mirror, Danny could see the bridge of his own nose. The intersection of the cross-hairs fell precisely between his image's eyes.

But the tall man didn't seem to be pleased. His triumphant expression changed slowly to one of shock. He said:

"You—you're not Berentz! Where is he? Speak up or I'll burn you down!"

"Tut," Danny said. "I never heard of him." He looked around. The small room might have been a laboratory, or perhaps a communications room or some kind of control room; it was hard to tell, since none of the apparatus was even slightly familiar to him. He doubted that even Todd would have been able to fathom the purpose of much of it. "I'm just a transient. Point that thing the other way, will you?"

The tall man lowered the gun indecisively—not far, but just enough to give Danny the satisfaction of seeing his belt-buckle instead of the bridge of his nose in the little mirror.

"Is this some trick?" he said hoarsely. "No one but Berentz had a translation permit. We have thought-sealed guarantees from kinetetrons on four planets, and a Prediction to boot. And instead of Berentz we get you! If you're making a Crossing illegally—"

"If what I'm doing is making a Crossing, it's a cinch to be illegal," Danny said. "But luckily I don't know what the hell you're talking about. Who is this Berentz?"

"He's image-librarian for the Geronticists, or he was until the Brotherhood got to him. Now he's charged with wholesale theft of alternate identities, and smuggling."

"Well, it sounds bad, all right," Danny said.

"It's bad, I assure you," said the tall man. "With all those alternates at their disposal, the Brothers will be able to infiltrate us at their own leisure and without our even knowing it—and since the Ophé affair, this is the last corner

227

of the galaxy that the Brothers don't own," he added bitterly. "Who are you, may I ask?"

Danny scratched his head. Any answer he could make might prove as nearly incomprehensible to the tall man as the tall man's talk was to Danny. On the other hand, in a sequence as dominated by the Brotherhood as the tall man had revealed this one to be, there was for the first time the possibility that it was also the prison of Todd, so that an ally might be invaluable.

He said cautiously, "I'm from another set of sequences."

"Oh. Why didn't you say so in the first place? You romantics, always looking for ultimate reality. If time travel were possible, you'd be doing that too. When are you going to learn that no sequence is stable?" He began to pace. "But you've upset my calculations, and Berentz is probably out of range by now. And there's no chance of help from Ophé—by this time that Tyrannosaur he's turned loose there will have the whole star cluster walled off."

Danny was interested in spite of himself. "Tyrannosaur? But they died out millions of years ago. I thought you said time travel was impossible."

"It is. There's a sequence some energy levels below this one where the dinosaurs never died, that's all—a highly improbable sequence, but that didn't prevent Berentz from raiding it."

"But they were supposed to have been stupid—brains the size of walnuts, and so on."

"They were," the tall man said moodily. "But that was milnes ago, when the time-rate didn't permit of physiochemical processes fast enough to sponsor intelligence. Put a man with the brains of a Caiden—"
228

"I beg your pardon?"

"Sorry—I forgot. No such person in your sequence, of course. He's a topological parapsychologist, a very difficult discipline. But put him back in the Carboniferous Age and he wouldn't think any better than a dinosaur. The energy level of the plenum as a whole at that time wouldn't have permitted it. But by the same token, the dinosaurs in the sequence where they've survived have a fair intelligence, despite the fact that their sauropsid circulatory system doesn't supply their brains with enough oxygenated blood to permit them to think very fast; and Berentz's Tyranno- saur is proving out as a very shrewd article. Oh, Berentz knew what he was doing. He should. He was our own top man until the Brothers corrupted him."

"I'm sorry," Danny said inadequately. "Not that it does you any good, but I didn't mess up your trap intentionally. That net you had around me—it can snatch a man who's teleporting himself, before he arrives where he wants to go?"

"Yes," the tall man said. "If the detector is exactly be- tween the origin and the intended destination. It took us months of calculation to get this ship out here, and I hate to think of the number of zeroes in the chances against your travelling in exactly the same line. However, I don't want to reproach you; you're not at fault."

The tall man sighed. Danny decided that he liked him. "Have you ever heard of a man named Todd in this sequence?"

"Todd? Hmm. Todd, Todd. It's a common name, after all, but still—"

"A parasychologist? If there's a Caiden here, there would probably be some connection between the two."

"Yes, I was going to say myself that I associated the two. Let's see now. It was—"

There was a sharp puff of air to Danny's left. Startled, Danny swung around.

Another man was standing in the low-ceilinged cabin. He was an exact duplicate of the tall, black-haired man, except for his expression, which did not look in the least downcast. And he had a duplicate of the tall man's gun.

He looked once at Danny and then away. "Hello, Zed," he said.

The first man looked him up and down with a contempt so freezing that Danny was grateful not to be the object of it. At last he said: "So you've stolen my alternate too, Berentz? You can congratulate yourself. Now we can never try you."

"I know," Zed's duplicate said. He grinned wolfishly. "The double jeopardy law. Too bad I can't shoot you, Zed; then things would be much simpler; of course I can still do a lot of damage. Maybe we can make an arrangement."

"Not now any more than last time," Zed said. "You'd better get out while the getting's good."

"And run into your snatcher? Not likely. Incidentally, Zed, the Brothers are homing on me, so they'll have this tin can of yours pinpointed within the half hour. Maybe you'd better think twice about coming to an agreement."

Berentz looked back at Danny. He did not seem to be seeing anything in particular; but he said, "You have quaint friends, Zed. I don't like witnesses."

He swung his gun on Danny and pulled the trigger.

The setting of the resonator prevented Danny from blocking the blast in any way, or taking any evasive action which could possibly have been fast enough. He had time only to shunt a part of the blast as it struck him, bleeding it back into the previous sequence, the one where there was no Earth.

Since that sequence had a lower energy level than Berentz's and Zed's, he later felt reasonably certain that Berentz had been instantly dragged by his gun hand back into that blazing chaos, but he had no time for so coherent a thought then.

The partial charge had already struck him—and had catapulted him into the next sequence.

SIX

There was nothing there.

There was not even blackness, though there was no light either. There was simply nothing at all, not even time. It had no more meaning nor reality than one's memory of the night's deep hours of sleep.

It was empty, in a way that no language had ever been set up to describe. Even a man who, like Zed, had been out between the stars would not have been able to describe such an emptiness—for space-time is a plenum, a fullness, awash with the steady beating of electromagnetic fields, contorted with matter, bound in its rigid metrical frame, crammed to bursting with positrons, expanding like a balloon with the pressure of its fullness.

Here, there was only empty space.

For a long time, nothing moved in Danny's mind but absolute desolation, so far beyond loneliness as to take it out of the realm of any normal human emotion. If he had any coherent thought at all, it was that Berentz had killed him; or—though it might have been days, years, centuries later when this occurred to him—that the charge from the gun had thrown him out of the sigma-sequence entirely, and into some sequence where the whole universe was nothing but a remote improbability.

The two came to the same thing in the end.

He turned helplessly in the emptiness. Eventually, he began to wonder, hopelessly, how he could know that he was turning. There were no reference points from which he could judge his motion.

But he turned. He could even feel a faint twinge of dizziness.

Dizziness; then, even here, not all his senses were utterly useless. The semi-circular canals of his inner ear were registering shifts in the inertia of the fluid they contained. His sense of balance was still working.

A tentative movement of his arm told him that kinesthesia, the sense of muscular position, was also still in operation; and so, evidently, were the pH sense and the other "interior" senses, the fifteen or more precise and delicate senses which kept the body going. Only his exterior senses, the famous five which most people think are all they own, were failing to register.

He was alive. That was at least a starting point. Furthermore, one of the interior senses which was still registering was able to tell him something of enormous importance about the nothingness outside himself. He felt dizzy; his sense of balance told him he was turning; and he would be getting no such sensation unless the fluid of his inner ear were still subject to centrifugal and Coriolis forces.

In the metrical field of space-time, those forces were not relative, but absolute—nothing could ever cancel them out, or mask them. Ergo, Danny was still in space-time—

And the apparent emptiness was an illusion.

The soundless, motionless, meaningless blackness was not characteristic, but imposed. There was no doubt in Danny's mind as to who had imposed it. This was his goal. The nothingness screamed the name of the Brotherhood to anyone who could understand it—even though it could be heard only with the inner ear. This was the PRS' ultimate aim: a sequence apparently emptied of all meaning, apparently emptied even of the very tissue of space-time. Without that tissue, that ground-matrix, the psi faculties were helpless.

The PRS, which alone knew how the condition was produced, could license favored people for access to other, more livable sequences, or it could deny access, at its own will. Above all, it could control the psi powers.

Probably this sequence was an end product: not what would prevail in the coming PRS sequence if Danny failed, but what the PRS would establish at the end of a long line of sequences.

And in it, Danny and Todd alike were trapped.

Nevertheless, there was a little hope. The resonator was still on the job, still holding Danny firmly to a single "frame" in this sequence exactly as it had done in all the others, and still maintaining the spread along the Planck

233

axis which would allow Danny to jump from this sequence too to another the moment the PRS allowed him to see which way to go. The PRS, of course, could simply leave him here; that would be final and fatal. But Danny was sure they lacked sufficient faith in their methods to feel themselves safe in trusting to nature. They would have to meddle.

Perhaps, again, he waited for centuries to see it proved. He could do nothing else but wait.

But in the end a minute glimmer of light began in the soundless void. It grew.

It became a glowing human face.

Mall's face.

chapter sixteen

TODD

The vast lips opened, and a soundless voice said, "Your death is somewhat delayed, Danny."

"I'm not dead yet," Danny said doggedly.

The glowing face smiled. "But you are," it said. "My predictions twice have shown you dead; once when you failed to show up with Hennessy, once when you entered the sigma-sequence. A third prediction of mine shows that you cannot escape from this space. You're dead, Danny."

"Your predictions are hogwash, and I'll give you two bits and a little device I happen to have here if you can get through that speech again *aloud*."

The face grew closer, the narrow eyes gleaming white-hot. "Mock if you like. An infirmity of speech isn't the same as an infirmity of the mind. Your friend Hennessy learned that the hard way. As for my predictions—prediction isn't an art practiced in a vacuum. The man who wants to see his predictions work must see to it that they do work. You've flouted two of mine; I mean to justify the two with a conspicuous success of the third. Or would you rather that I left you here?"

235

"Try it."

Mall did not answer. His face was now all that Danny could see, out to the very edges of his cone of vision. Something lethal was gathering in the eyes.

But Danny was remembering. He carried with him, even here, the desolation and terror of a world where there were no men, and the lonely savagery of a carrion bird seeking its last victim. A soldier on a high tower said, "You crazy fool, you'll be dead anyhow in a—" and his voice broke off, and was replaced by the voice of a thing like a mantis with caterpillar treads, murmuring, "A formulation out of the matrix . . . disturbing factor . . . cancel . . . junk me for it . . ." In a gap instinct with raw energy, the roiling of the Bethé reaction, that same hydrogenbomb reaction which had wiped out the soldier, stirred a thin gas that had once been the Earth; and a hawk-nosed, black-haired man reminded Danny that no sequence was ultimately stable.

It added up. It had to; it was all concentrated by the resonator into a single frame. In sum it was the most enormous psychic potential ever accumulated by a single human being, and up to now it had lacked only a target.

Danny's hatred of everything the PRS stood for, and the vast face of Mall peeping through the enforced blackness, gave him his target. He gathered the bolt and launched it.

The inane sequence shook. The glowing face twisted in agony. It receded almost instantly to a pinpoint of light.

"Danny! *Danny!* Hold him there! I'll be through to you in a minute!"

Todd's voice—

236

But the pinpoint of light refused to wink out. Danny could feel Mall's presence, gathering itself for some unimaginable blow of its own. Mall had been able to beat down Sean and Danny together once before; he was still alive somewhere. He was coming back.

The darkness began to rock. Around the distant not-star, and around Danny, an invisible and basic storm seemed to be raging, as if the very metrical structure of space were being tortured, its geodesics twisted like the strands in a dishcloth. How the terrific stresses were being applied, or from where, it was impossible to know.

Mall's face grew again in the invisible turmoil. This time he was not shouting for Sir Lewis and Schaum and the others. To handle Danny alone, he had no need of help. His eyes burned destruction; he was the only source of light in the universe, and he radiated death.

And then, abruptly, he was not.

A sound like the ripping of metal screamed out somewhere behind the swelling head. A jagged line of light, like lightning frozen in mid-stroke, split the blackness. Against it, Mall's head—and not only his head, but his shoulders and chest—were not light, but dark, making him seem considerably less gigantic.

The split widened rapidly, now silhouetting Mall's whole figure. Then the divided sides of the sable curtain were torn aside entirely, and light and reality spilled through.

They were in the garret. Mall stood no more than fifteen feet away, looking over his own shoulder in furious, arrested astonishment. Behind him, before the open door of the apparatus-jammed room which Danny had seen once

237

before, was Todd, astride a massive and incredible machine. The device was half searchlight and half siege gun,
and Todd was mounted on it in a metal bucket seat, his
feet in things like bicycle pedals. The whole apparatus had
the look of having been put together with the most frantic
haste a fanatically careful technician could muster.

"Danny! *Hold him!*"

The resonator was hot in Danny's hand. Somehow he
got the cover off, and the controls turned to highest amplification. The last of the blackness leaked out of things, and
the garret became stable and solid. The sequences he had
visited took their places in his mind in their proper, frac-
tional reality. That reality was partial—but it was real.

"Hold him!"

The sixfold impulse, backed by all the power of Sean's
resonator, slammed into Mall's straining body. He turned
white under his red hair and staggered, fighting for a foot-
hold on the floorboards of the attic.

But the blow was not enough. Mall began to come
across the floor toward Danny, one painful step after another. A counter-pressure played back from him around
Danny, impossibly strong, and hot with murder.

Todd struggled with his machine. Then he said, "Ah."

The device jerked and swung down to bear on Mall.
From its muzzle or lens—whichever it was—a fountain of
dancing lights issued, a vortex of little flames.

For an instant Mall was drenched in that impossible
fountain. Then his figure was obscured, as if a second Mall
stood there, interpenetrating the first. Then there were
four interpenetrating figures, all somehow less solid than
238

a human body; then eight; then sixteen; then thirty-two . . .

Shadow-figures of Mall bled away from his rigid body by the hundreds, by the thousands, evaporating into the natural shadows of the garret.

After a while there was nothing left of Mall.

Todd shut his machine off. Danny adjusted the resonator again and returned it to his pocket with violently shaking hands.

"Beautiful, Danny," Todd said. "How you got up here I can't fathom, and what you did to him to make him hold still I suppose I'll never know. But you did it."

"But what in god's name did you do? Where's Mall?"

"Scattered," Todd said calmly. He dismounted from his machine, awkwardly but with dignity. "He has one integer now in every sequence, but no concentration on the main line or anywhere else. He's only a spread of characteristics now—a matrix in probability. He can never be assembled again."

Danny looked around the garret. It was empty except for Todd and the machine.

"We'll have to find Sean," he said at last. "But, Dr. Todd, where did they have you? When I heard your voice, I would have sworn you were in that empty space."

"I was," Todd said, "but not in the same way you were. I think you were in the end of the sequence; I was at the beginning, where the cancelling field that made the darkness hadn't been generally established yet.

"They were incredibly stupid, Danny. They had figured that I wouldn't be able to operate directly with the serial universe—I have no talent for it, it seems—but they forgot
239

that I could assemble machinery to act for me, just as they had done in setting up their trap in the stairwell.

"So they hid me in their own laboratories, at the beginning of their sequence, which had been picked as 'theirs' because every factor in it seemed to favor them. It was the worst thing they could have done. I'll never be a psi-man, but you'd be surprised at the way I can throw the psi forces about when I have proper equipment!"

"Nothing surprises me," Danny said. "Not any more. You're the man who deserves the pat on the back, Dr. Todd. You've solved the problem of psychic fission that Sean's group has been working on, apparently for years."

"Oh?" The parapsychologist looked pleased and crest-fallen at the same time. "I was going to call it the Todd Effect. Well, perhaps the whole thing is better forgotten. I wouldn't care to see a really perfected machine of this type turned on a crowd at low power. There would be mental disorders and violence of an unprecedented sort."

"That was Sean's conclusion too."

Todd looked regretfully at the machine. "Perhaps it had better be left in the psi-men's hands—or even destroyed for rediscovery by a wiser age. Scattering Mall fused most of its innards . . . Hmm. Shall we agree to forget it, Danny?"

"Tentatively," Danny said. "I'll want Sean's decision, if he's still alive. We'll have to find him. We still have to bring the sequence Sean wanted to see founded onto the main line."

"We just did," Todd said. "This is it."

For a moment Danny stood stunned. "Are you sure?" he said at last. "Are you sure we're even on the main line right now?"

"Yes, to both," Todd said. "The destruction of Mall reduces the PRS sequence to a very low order of probability. He was their key man. I confess I had no hope of your getting this far, or of your being able to pin Mall down for me if you did. All my struggles with the T—with psychic fission were at a venture, in hopes of providing myself with a weapon. Finding Mall in range of it was considerably beyond my best hopes.

"And the energy I expended in scattering him, plus the energy I expended in building the machine in the first place, and in thinking about it beforehand—real energy, every erg of it a tap on the PRS' headstone—has established the sequence your friend was fighting for, very solidly on the main line."

The scientist patted the now-useless machine affectionately. "This thing was intended only as a memory-tapper, to drag what I'd learned out of me—a sort of polished version of our barber's-chair-cum-encephalograph. They didn't expect you to get so far, either, or I'm sure they'd never have left me alone with it for an instant."

"I don't know," Danny said thoughtfully. "They tend to think of things in terms of the uses they were designed for, and not in terms of what they might be converted to. It was the way they thought, and I think I know why. If you stick yourself off in a sequence where your wishes are *already* fact, you aren't going to be able to foresee actual outcomes, not even with the psi powers. No wonder Mall's 'predictions' didn't work out. They weren't really predictions at all—just projected wishes."

He turned. The stairway to the first floor was before him. It was just a simple stairway, with nothing left to show that it had been a well of confusion a few minutes ago. A smell of burned insulation and hot ozone came up it. Danny began to laugh.

"Whatever it was that created that field, it's burned out but good," he said. "Let's go down, Dr. Todd—we've still got a score to settle with Sir Lewis."

They went down the stairs. Danny took each of the first few steps with care and a little apprehension, though he was reasonably sure that they were only simple steps now. By the time he reached the bottom, however, he had almost gotten used to using stairs again.

But Sir Lewis was not to be found, and neither was anybody else. The downstairs rooms were deserted. Danny prowled through them. Though there was plenty of evidence that the PRS men had left in extreme haste, he could not find what he was seeking.

In the largest room of all, the nap of the carpet was pressed flat in several spots, in regular rectangles which were a lot lighter in color than the rest of the rug. Danny scuffed at one of them with the toe of his shoe.

"Those are what I really wanted," he said gloomily. "Their files. Sean told me that the PRS had been playing the market and that they were responsible for the Wheat scandal. But I'm the boy that's going to have to prove it to the FBI—and the files are gone."

Todd nodded sympathetically. "Tough, Danny. But maybe we can locate them. I'll try the cellar."

Danny stood silently where he was. He was sure the files could not be in the building, though he welcomed Todd's sympathy.

Danny.

242

Danny started. The covered, "underground" tone of the mental voice told him at once that some psi-man was opening a coded thought to him; yet to his deep disappointment, it was not Sean.

Is that you, Mr. Taylor?

Cartier Taylor, yes. Come have a beer with me when you've time. Right now use ESP on your problem. Remember that matter is electronic and that electrons think—I'm not so fussy about my terminology as Sean. But try it. They should remember what you want to know.

Thanks, I will. Where is Sean? Is he alive?

Sean is where you are. I can't place him more exactly; but he's alive or I wouldn't be able to pick him up. Get to him fast, though; he's in a bad way. And congratulations, Danny, to you and Todd.

The voice cut out. Danny tried to put himself into contact with the electrons of the carpet and the nearby wall. At first it was a flat failure; he was used to dealing with electrons only with PK, and obviously that would be useless here. The whole notion of using ESP on the electronic level was hard to grasp.

The resonator helped, unexpectedly. A picture began to come through. The filing cabinets had stood here, as he already knew from the impressions in the carpet; the electronic "memories" gave him shadowy impressions of them from previous frames.

Then, dimly at first, the same memory pattern began to come through to him from some other room, somewhere quite distant. Another and very familiar electronic "set" or area was recording the presence of the cabinets, and holding it faithfully in focus for anyone with the psi-

243

senses to detect it. Doubtless Taylor, had he been present, could have worked out the answer in an instant, but for Danny it was as tantalizing as an almost-remembered word which would not fall into place. He recognized the new location, but he could not get the picture all the way through—

"Danny, I'll have to disturb you a minute."

"Uhm?"

"Come over here and take a look at this." Todd was standing in the doorway to the cellar stairs. With a sudden chill of anticipation, Danny followed him down the steps.

"Is this the man you call Sean?"

Danny didn't answer. He could not speak; he could not even nod.

Sean was lying on a collapsible pallet toward the back of the cement-walled room, near the oil-burner. His face was gentle and no longer sardonic; even the slight rictus of death made his white face look more composed and content.

Danny swallowed harshly, and Todd took his arm.

"I'm sorry, Danny. You loved him, didn't you?"

"He—was a great man, Dr. Todd. Or he would have been if they had let him live." His mouth set bitterly. "I'm surprised that they didn't take the body with them. I'm going to place charges against Sir Lewis as an accessory."

"How can you do that? I gather that you were a witness, but one isn't enough. And from the looks of the wound, they must have gotten him with some weapon you could never explain in a court."

"It could just as easily have been a hot poker," Danny
244

said savagely. "They would've taken him away if they could. They'll be sorry they didn't."

Todd bent over the body and lifted it, at first gently, and then with all his strength. Though his thin arms were wiry and strong, Sean did not move.

Todd straightened, panting. "There's your reason," he said, rubbing his shoulder muscles. "He can't be lifted. He must have done something to his mass before he died; he has about ten tons of inertia right now, at a guess." He shook his head. "I'd give a lot to know how he got the added inertia without upping his weight."

Danny tried it himself. The body would not move, not even by a fraction of an inch; even pushing back Shean's eyelashes was as difficult as bending the teeth of a comb.

Taylor had said that Sean was not dead, but "in a bad way"—as fas as Taylor could tell from where he was. Yet Sean was obviously dead.

Suddenly Danny guessed the truth. Carefully, he explored the dead man's mind.

The key was deeply buried, almost masked by the rapidly progressing, far advanced disintegration of Sean's brain-cells. But once he hit it, the tight knot of PK energy was unmistakable. It was tuned to Danny, and to no one else. The moment he reached it, it dissipated; and Danny felt again, although far more weakly, that passing wave of identity, of a person becoming an un-person and a part of the general wave-flux of the universe, that he had felt at Sean's death.

"Dr. Todd—"

Todd tightened his grip on Danny's arm and waited.

"Thanks. Try it now, will you? I'd—rather not."

245

"Certainly." Todd moved Sean's hand experimentally. "Yes, that does it. What did you do? Had he locked himself down here for you?"

"Yes."

"How?"

"I don't know. Maybe we'll find out later. You've solved one of his problems yourself, the psychic fission effect, and he expected you to do so. Maybe he expects you to solve the other problem too. Anyhow we'll all be working on it from now on, now that we know what it must have been."

"What?" Todd said quietly.

"Death," Danny said.

After a while, Todd said, "Yes. That would be it. Danny, we've a lot to learn."

Danny turned his attention back to the rectangular clean spots on the carpet upstairs, his mind reaching again for the electronic "set" of the filing cabinets. Was it the PRS' brownstone? It was a logical guess; but after only a few seconds he knew it was a wrong one. Why was the new location so maddeningly familiar?

And then he had it.

The files were in his own apartment. The PRS had had nothing to do with their vanishment; Sean must have stolen them and teleported them to Danny's rooms the moment he had entered the hide-out. Sean had seen what was coming, and had acted accordingly. Small wonder that the PRS had cut and run when Mall had been dispersed, and Danny and Todd freed of the last possible PRS trap.

"Dr. Todd, I think we're going on a truck ride, if I can

come to an agreement with the engine. Help me upstairs with Sean."

"I will do nothing of the kind," Todd said. "I am well-preserved but no longer young. You, on the other hand, are a psi-man with a fully operative PK center, and I'm considering hiring you to do all my heavy lifting."

"Sorry; I forgot. It's all pretty new yet. Let's go, then."

chapter seventeen

MARLA

The reception the two men got at Danny's apartment was nothing short of royal. The place was full of FBI men, and the FBI men's hands were full of papers. The FBI men had a male secretary with them, who was being kept very busy making lists.

The agent who had visited Danny before smiled up at him from the big chair. "A neat trick," he said, indicating the cabinets. "How did you do it?"

"I had help," Danny said. "I gather that I'm not under arrest any more?"

"Technically, technically," the FBI man said, waving the matter away. "You did violate your bond, which you'll have to explain. In this case the results are what counts; this stuff here will satisfy the Grand Jury for a long, long time, and Uncle Sam has discovered a few interesting things, too. I think the American assets of Consolidated Warfare are due for a quick freeze."

"What, another scare on the market?"

"We've had it," the agent said, a trifle grimly. "A big

one. It's a part of our case; how could the dissolution of a nut-cult affect the munitions market? Obviously it couldn't; but it did. Oh, it's juicy, and all Uncle Sam is worried about now is the choice of a court to try it in. We're going to need a judge with the openest mind in all history."

Danny's eyes widened. "You mean you're going to bring out the ESP angle?"

"Certainly we are. Evidently it hasn't occurred to you, Mr. Caiden, that the military security of this country isn't worth a nickel unless we can get some equivalent of the Manhattan Project at work on these new psychical forces at once. Unfortunately it's too late to clamp a real security lid over them; we're driven to the opposite extreme of bringing it all out in the open, partly because the stuff is so fantastic that we couldn't get an appropriation for a secret project, and partly because of the existence of this organized international group."

"Whew," Danny said. "And I thought I was going to have to lie myself blue in the face in order to keep from sounding crazy to you people. What convinced you so fast?"

"I was here," the agent said, unhappily, "when these cabinets snapped into existence, right out of thin air. I have to believe what I see, especially when I have to push around a broken toe to remind me of it. I hope you're not still mad at me—or, if you are, I hope your aim doesn't improve with practice."

"I didn't send the cabinets," Danny said. "The man who did was a friend of mine who was murdered by one of the PRS men. I've got the body downstairs in a truck I stole. Can I prefer charges against Sir Lewis Carter as an accomplice?"

The FBI man groaned. "I rue the day I took this case on—just a simple little anti-trust case . . . Mr. Caiden, I just don't know. I suppose you can, after you get the kinks ironed out of your own life. Don't tell me how you stole this truck now, because I couldn't stand it. Do you know where we can lay hands on Sir Lewis?"

"No," Danny said. "And you couldn't keep him in jail for ten seconds once you caught him."

"He's not a teleport, according to the society's records," the agent said. "Just a telepath."

"He has friends, though. Some of them are teleports." Danny remembered the resonator. He took it out and handed it over. "I won't be needing this for a while," he added. "Dr. Todd can show you how to build more, after which I'd appreciate your giving it back to me. It's kept a better man than Sir Lewis in the pokey."

"You're bragging," Todd said, returning at this juncture from a complete circuit of the apartment. "But you're right. Danny, I find something strange here. With all this official joy over our reappearance, you'd think they might have arranged to have had your young lady on hand. I suppose the legal mind isn't given to human emotions as we know them, however."

"She's here," Danny said, grinning. "She's been hiding in the closet, waiting for me to ask where she is. Right now she's furious because it's been ten minutes and I haven't mentioned her yet—"

The closet door flew open. Marla stalked out, her hands on her hips, her eyes hot. "You and your damned trickery!"

she spat. "How could a woman have any secrets from a man like that?"

"A woman with a guilty conscience has no business dallying with a telepath," Danny said. "Even in the pursuit of knowledge. He's likely to learn more than she is. Right now, for instance, I wish you'd get a little madder, because what's actually on your mind is doing terrible things to my illusions."

"Danny Caiden, you can just go—go—"

She seemed unable to think of anything that might prove fatal to Danny. She stomped out of the room instead. Danny followed, closing the apartment door behind himself. At the head of the stairs she paused indecisively, and Danny caught her by the elbow.

"I'm sorry, Marla. Really. I was teasing you, that's all."

"Prove it," she said.

"How? Shall I go back inside and throw some furniture around?"

"No, goddam it," she said. "Do something simple that a girl can understand, for once, instead of scaring her into fits."

Danny made a hollow tube of his tongue and made a noise like a turtledove. As an afterthought, he drew from the pocket of her jacket the glass tube from one of his emperor-sized cigarettes, and with it made a noise like a steamboat whistle.

Marla's eyes only became more dangerous.

"Well," Danny said, "I can think of only one other expedient." He grasped her, hard, by the shoulders, and pulled her toward him.

She punched him, promptly, just under his bottom

251

rib, with considerable force. He let go of her with an angry yelp.

"You egg-head," she said. "What were you going to do—kiss me on the forehead like a brother?"

She put her arms around his neck, and her thighs pressed against his. Her mouth was hot and sweet.

Some moments later, Marla removed his arms firmly, and stepped back against the wall. "That's better," she said. "But you've got to realize, Danny, that I'm dead serious about this psychic business. It's got to stop. I have just as many nasty thoughts as the next woman and I want them to be my own."

"I don't go around reading people's thoughts except in emergencies, Marla," Danny said. "I wouldn't have picked you up at all, there in the closet, if I hadn't been damned worried about where you were and why you weren't on hand. What I said about what you were thinking after you came out of the closet was teasing and nothing more, just like I said before."

"That isn't good enough—don't you understand? I'd never *know*. I'm scared of it. When I want to be heard, I speak aloud. Living with you would deprive me of any choice of remaining silent, no matter how good your intentions were. I know I couldn't resist the temptation to take a peek occasionally, if I could. I defy anybody on the face of the Earth to resist a temptation that sizable."

"Why resist it?" Danny said eagerly. "Marla, there's nothing abnormal about the psi faculties. Everybody has them in some degree, and I think you've got a large helping. I can show you how to use them, and Todd

252

can help, too. Then we'd be even; it would be a convention of privacy between us. Each of us can see, but whatever our curiosity about someone, we satisfy it only under conditions laid down by the other. Married people don't peep through bathroom keyholes in their own homes, after all."

"No," Marla said. "I don't want any part of it. If you really want me to marry you, you'll have to give it up, Danny. I don't want to be a stinker about it, but I can't help myself. It scares me too much."

"How do you give up an ability?" Danny asked, reasonably. "It would be like agreeing not to see without at the same time giving up my eyes. I'm not even sure it could be done. Surgery would be the only recourse, and even there it would probably make an idiot of me, now that full cortical connections have been established. And the surgeon would have to find the spot in my brain where the master formula is and extirpate that; he could slash everything else in my head, but if he missed that, I'd still be a psi-man."

Marla said nothing. Danny added dubiously, "You see how it is. But we could make the agreement. And I could be careful not to throw furniture around or teleport anything or carry the garbage out any way but by hand—no psychokinesis or ESP to be used around you, that'd be the law. And it's highly probable that I won't have a chance at a sigma-sequence ever again—"

Marla stamped her foot and turned her back on him.

Danny stood for a moment, swallowing, in a gray fog of desolation. He was about to turn away when something

253

came to him, something so desperate that it left him shaking.

Nothing he had ever had to do, nothing he had ever suffered, no fear he had ever felt, cost him so much as this; but it was the only thing left to be done.

Carefully, with the utmost precision, and with the utmost relentlessness toward himself, he constructed in his own brain a phantom brain, an electronic "set" which duplicated his every attitude, his every memory, his every concept, his every impulse, even his every reflex and every buried circuitous drive which was hidden from his own conscious sight. He left out nothing: the sessions in the bathroom with the book; the theft from the purse of his mother's guest; the pricking of the fat boy's treasured blimp-balloon; the tethered dog whirling with B-B shot from a nearby window; every minutely specific thought he had ever had about Marla; every lie; every disgrace; every defeat. Everything.

And when he had the phantom construct complete, he moved it delicately out of his own brain and into Marla's.

She seemed to shrink the moment it touched her. "I'll kill you," she said tonelessly. "I'll kill you if you touch my mind again. Oh! Oh god I'm going crazy. Oh. I'll kill you. I'll kill you."

She put her hands to her face.

And so it had all come to nothing. An old motto said that familiarity breeds contempt. Danny's attempt to breed love from it had collapsed; and he knew that he should have expected nothing else. As he had built up the phantom image of himself, his loathing for himself had grown too, until he was almost ready to wonder why he should be allowed to live. Why had he expected Marla to find the picture any more attractive? He had simply committed another stupidity.

Marla seemed to be crying. He hesitated a moment longer, and then went back into the apartment. The FBI man looked at him brightly.

"No soap?" he said. "That's tough, Mr. Caiden. That little girl has a mind of her own, as I seem to remember."

"*Shut up.*"

The FBI man shut up, but he shifted in the big chair and began handling his papers with a certain inattention. It was painfully obvious that he wanted to go out into the hall and re-try his own luck.

Then Danny heard her calling, in a small voice, through the door.

"Danny. Danny."

"I'm here," he said.

"Danny—*look at me.*"

The FBI man leered pleasantly. Danny didn't care. His ESP center had picked up Marla upon the instant; and found an enormous gift.

The gift of confidence.

Her picture of herself was blurred and incomplete, since she lacked training, but it was horribly frank. Some of it was very hard to take; it fought viciously with prejudices and conventions Danny had been accepting through his pores almost since his birth.

But it was as all there as Marla could make it. She had given him the same gift he had offered her, to the utmost of her power. No wonder she had resisted and

255

cried when Danny had forced his confidence upon her; but she was giving it back.

"Marla—" he cried aloud.

Danny wait—just a minute. Come out and kiss me again. But—

Her thoughts blurred; she was having a hard time controlling the flow of concepts, a flow she had never had to think of before as a form of communication. But eventually she found what she wanted to say.

But this time please open the door before you walk through it!